EVERYMAN, I will go with thee,

and be thy guide,

In thy most need to go by thy side

JEROME K. JEROME

Born at Walsall, Staffordshire, in 1859, the son of a lay preacher. Educated at a school in London, then was a railway clerk and part-time actor. Editor of *The Idler*, 1892. Ambulance driver for the French Red Cross in the First World War. Died in 1927.

JEROME K. JEROME

Three Men
on the Bummel

INTRODUCTION BY
D. C. BROWNING, M.A., B.LITT.

Dent London Melbourne Toronto
EVERYMAN'S LIBRARY
Dutton New York

No 188 Hardback ISBN 0 460 00188 4
No 1188 Paperback ISBN 0 460 01188 x

INTRODUCTION

JEROME KLAPKA JEROME was born on 2nd May 1859, at Walsall in Staffordshire, where his father, Jerome Clapp Jerome, was a lay preacher. His middle name forms a puzzle at the outset, for it had no connection with his father's, but was that of a famous Hungarian general who was an intimate friend of the family. To prevent confusion with his father the boy was usually called Luther at home. While he was still a child the family moved to Poplar, and at school in London he had Willett, the originator of daylight saving, as a class-mate. By the time he had reached the age of fifteen Jerome had lost both his parents and found life in lodgings on his railway clerk's pay a hard struggle, but was able to supplement this by spare-time acting, for he was very fond of the theatre. His first book, *On the Stage—and Off*, brought him only £5, but he was already winning popularity as a writer when in 1888 he married Georgina Henrietta Stanley. Next year his amusing *Idle Thoughts of an Idle Fellow* appeared by instalments in the magazine *Home Chimes*, and was followed there by the famous *Three Men in a Boat*. In 1892 he was joint editor of *The Idler*, and in the following year started his own weekly, *To-day*, with R. L. Stevenson's 'Ebb Tide' as the serial, but a costly lawsuit brought it to an end. Meanwhile he was celebrated both as playwright and as novelist. Of his plays the most famous is *The Passing of the Third Floor Back*, a kind of modern morality with characters named Cheat, Slut, Rogue, and Cad; incidentally, it has twice been performed, like the old moralities, in a church. Of his novels *Paul Kelver* is usually reckoned the best. When the First World War broke out he offered himself for active service, and when he was rejected as being over age he joined the French Red Cross as an ambulance driver. To one of his sensitivity the horror of the scenes he witnessed was heart-rending and undoubtedly shortened his life. He died on 14th June 1927, and is buried in the churchyard of Ewelme, a pretty village in the Chilterns.

The river was a favourite resort of Jerome's; like his contemporary, Kenneth Grahame, he loved 'messing about in boats,' and it is not surprising that his most famous book should have the Thames for its background. The real paradox is that it was not planned as a humorous book at all, but was meant to be an historical and topographical account of the river, entitled 'The Story of the Thames.' Fortunately for posterity, cheerfulness, not to say frivolity, kept breaking in, and the amusing passages were such a success that when the 'chunks of history' turned up they were ruthlessly cut by the editor of *Home Chimes*, where the story was running as a serial. The three men, it should be explained, were quite genuine. 'Harris' was Carl Hentschel, a Pole who was usually taken for a German; 'George' was George Wingrave; and Jerome himself made the third of the trio who used to take the train to Richmond and spend their Sundays on the river together. The dog Montmorency is also an actual character, and his discomfiture when he wrestled with the boiling kettle is founded on a real incident, just as the three men's exploits were based on the actual experiences of Jerome and his two friends. The story was a tremendous success not only in this country but in America, where more than a million copies were sold. Unfortunately, as British copyright was not yet protected in that country, the author got nothing from the transatlantic sales. In England copies went so fast that the publisher thought 'the public must eat them,' and the new type of humour became firmly established. As late as 1956 a film version of the book was produced with success.

Three Men on the Bummel, a sort of sequel, appeared in 1900. The title must be puzzling to many readers, for 'bummel' will not be found in English dictionaries. In typically tantalizing fashion Jerome waits till the last paragraph of the book to explain that it is a German word meaning a journey without any definite object; 'ramble' is perhaps the nearest English equivalent. The book describes a cycling tour through the Black Forest, and the same characters appear as are in the earlier work, only they are rather older and have no dog this time; two of them are married, and there is a good deal of joking at the outset about the problem of getting away from their wives. The book has many digressions; indeed, the first chapter is largely devoted to the account of another journey that never really got started. The whole is a rambling account of a rambling holiday, with delightful word-pictures of the Germany of sixty years ago, before two wars bred hostility and suspicion between the countries. Like most sequels, it has been compared unfavourably with its parent story, but it was only a little less celebrated than *Three Men in a Boat*, and was for long used as a school book in Germany.

It is an obvious temptation to criticize Jerome's books as old-fashioned, 'Victorian,' and out of date, for admittedly the world he writes of is very different from ours. The London of last century seems now very far away. Its streets were crowded with horse-buses, 'four-wheelers,' and jingling hansoms. The bicycle was the fastest thing on the road, for the law that motor vehicles must be preceded by a man carrying a red flag was not repealed till 1896. And to a post-war generation the money values are fantastic. Mrs Jerome, the writer's mother, notes in her diary: 'Coals have been eight shillings a ton. It is a fearful prospect.' In his autobiography Jerome tells us that as a clerk earning twopence-halfpenny an hour he found lunch a constant problem; you could hardly get a meal under ninepence, and you had to leave a penny for the waitress. When he married, their house in Chelsea Gardens, with five rooms and kitchen, had a rent of fourteen shillings a week; and income tax had reached the iniquitous figure of eightpence in the pound. It seems almost like another planet. But while conditions change, human nature remains the same. The counterparts to Jerome's shirt-sleeved pipe-smoking young clerks may still be seen any fine day on the reaches between Richmond and Kingston, and the pranks they play on one another will have changed little in the new century. Wit is quickly outdated, humour is everlasting. The jokes of Jerome's immortal three may sometimes be crude and lacking in intellectual refinement, but their appeal does not lessen with the passing years. And behind the author's ironical comments there is always a vein of sound if whimsical philosophy which gives his most extravagant flights of fancy a value all their own.

D. C. BROWNING.

1957.

CONTENTS

BIBLIOGRAPHY

The following is a list of Jerome K. Jerome's principal works:

FICTION. *Three Men in a Boat*, 1889; *Told After Supper*, 1891; *John Inger-
field and Other Stories*, 1894; *Sketches in Lavender, Blue, and Green*, 1897;
Three Men on the Bummel, 1900; *The Observations of Henry*, 1901; *Paul
Kelver*, 1902; *Tommy and Co.*, 1904; *The Passing of the Third Floor Back and
Other Stories*, 1907; *The Angel and the Author*, 1908; *Malvina of Brittany*,
1916; *Anthony John*, 1923.

PLAYS. *Barbara*, 1886; *Miss Hobbs*, 1899; *The Passing of the Third Floor
Back*, 1907; *Fanny and the Servant Problem*, 1908; *The Master of Mrs
Chilvers*, 1911; *The Soul of Nicholas Snyders*, 1927.

MISCELLANEOUS WRITINGS. *On the Stage—and Off*, 1885; *Stageland*, 1889;
Idle Thoughts of an Idle Fellow, 1889; *Diary of a Pilgrimage*, 1891; *Novel
Notes*, 1893; *Second Thoughts of an Idle Fellow*, 1898; *Tea Table Talk*, 1903;
Idle Ideas in 1905, 1905; *They and I*, 1909; *All Roads Lead to Calvary*, 1919;
My Life and Times, 1926.

LIFE. Alfred Moss: *Jerome K. Jerome, his Life and Work*, 1929.

NOTE

The illustrations by L. Raven Hill are those which appeared
in the first edition.

CHAPTER I

'WHAT we want,' said Harris, 'is a change.'

At this moment the door opened, and Mrs Harris put her head
in to say that Ethelbertha had sent her to remind me that we
must not be late getting home because of Clarence. Ethelbertha,
I am inclined to think, is unnecessarily nervous about the children. As a matter of fact, there was nothing wrong with the
child whatever. He had been out with his aunt that morning;
and if he looks wistfully at a pastry-cook's window she takes him
inside and buys him cream buns and 'maids-of-honour' until he
insists that he has had enough, and politely, but firmly, refuses to
eat another anything. Then, of course, he wants only one
helping of pudding at lunch, and Ethelbertha thinks he is
sickening for something. Mrs Harris added that it would be as
well for us to come upstairs soon, on our own account also, as
otherwise we should miss Muriel's rendering of 'The Mad
Hatter's Tea Party,' out of *Alice in Wonderland*. Muriel is
Harris's second, age eight: she is a bright, intelligent child; but I
prefer her myself in serious pieces. We said we would finish
our cigarettes and follow almost immediately; we also begged her
not to let Muriel begin until we arrived. She promised to hold
the child back as long as possible, and went. Harris, as soon as
the door was closed, resumed his interrupted sentence.

'You know what I mean,' he said, 'a complete change.'

The question was how to get it.

George suggested 'business.' It was the sort of suggestion
George would make. A bachelor thinks a married woman
doesn't know enough to get out of the way of a steam-roller. I

1

knew a young fellow once, an engineer, who thought he would go to Vienna 'on business.' His wife wanted to know 'what business?' He told her it would be his duty to visit the mines in the neighbourhood of the Austrian capital, and to make reports. She said she would go with him; she was that sort of woman. He tried to dissuade her: he told her that a mine was no place for a beautiful woman. She said she felt that herself, and that therefore she did not intend to accompany him down the shafts; she would see him off in the morning, and then amuse herself until his return, looking round the Vienna shops, and buying a few things she might want. Having started the idea, he did not see very well how to get out of it; and for ten long summer days he did visit the mines in the neighbourhood of Vienna, and in the evening wrote reports about them, which she posted for him to his firm, who didn't want them.

I should be grieved to think that either Ethelbertha or Mrs Harris belonged to that class of wife, but it is as well not to overdo 'business'—it should be kept for cases of real emergency.

'No,' I said, 'the thing is to be frank and manly. I shall tell Ethelbertha that I have come to the conclusion a man never values happiness that is always with him. I shall tell her that, for the sake of learning to appreciate my own advantages as I know they should be appreciated, I intend to tear myself away from her and the children for at least three weeks. I shall tell her,' I continued, turning to Harris, 'that it is you who have shown me my duty in this respect; that it is to you we shall owe——'

Harris put down his glass rather hurriedly.

'If you don't mind, old man,' he interrupted, 'I'd really rather you didn't. She'll talk it over with my wife, and—well, I should not be happy, taking credit that I do not deserve.'

'But you do deserve it,' I insisted; 'it was your suggestion.'

'It was you gave me the idea,' interrupted Harris again. 'You know you said it was a mistake for a man to get into a groove, and that unbroken domesticity cloyed the brain.'

'I was speaking generally,' I explained.

'It struck me as very apt,' said Harris. 'I thought of repeating it to Clara; she has a great opinion of your sense, I know. I am sure that if——'

'We won't risk it,' I interrupted, in my turn; 'it is a delicate matter, and I see a way out of it. We will say George suggested the idea.'

There is a lack of genial helpfulness about George that it sometimes vexes me to notice. You would have thought he would
have welcomed the chance of assisting two old friends out of a
dilemma; instead, he became disagreeable.

'You do,' said George, 'and I shall tell them both that my
original plan was that we should make a party—children and all;
that I should bring my aunt, and that we should hire a charming
old château I know of in Normandy, on the coast, where the
climate is peculiarly adapted to delicate children, and the milk
such as you do not get in England. I shall add that you overrode
that suggestion, arguing we should be happier by ourselves.'

With a man like George kindness is of no use; you have to be
firm.

'You do,' said Harris, 'and I, for one, will close with the
offer. We will just take that château. You will bring your aunt
—I will see to that—and we will have a month of it. The
children are all fond of you; J. and I will be nowhere. You've
promised to teach Edgar fishing; and it is you who will have
to play wild beasts. Since last Sunday Dick and Muriel have
talked of nothing else but your hippopotamus. We will picnic
in the woods—there will only be eleven of us—and in the
evenings we will have music and recitations. Muriel is master
of six pieces already, as perhaps you know; and all the other
children are quick studies.'

George climbed down—he has no real courage—but he did
not do it gracefully. He said that if we were mean and cowardly
and false-hearted enough to stoop to such a shabby trick, he
supposed he couldn't help it; and that if I didn't intend to finish
the whole bottle of claret myself, he would trouble me to spare
him a glass. He also added, somewhat illogically, that it really
did not matter, seeing both Ethelbertha and Mrs Harris were
women of sense who would judge him better than to believe for a
moment that the suggestion emanated from him.

This little point settled, the question was: What sort of a
change?

Harris, as usual, was for the sea. He said he knew a yacht,
just the very thing—one that we could manage by ourselves; no
skulking lot of lubbers loafing about, added to the expense and
taking away from the romance. Give him a handy boy, he
would sail it himself. We knew that yacht, and we told him so;
we had been on it with Harris before. It smells of bilge-water
and greens to the exclusion of all other scents; no ordinary sea air

can hope to head against it.   So far as sense of smell is concerned, one might be spending a week in Limehouse Hole.
There is no place to get out of the rain; the saloon is ten feet by
four, and half of that is taken up by a stove, which falls to pieces
when you go to light it.   You have to take your bath on deck,
and the towel blows overboard just as you step out of the tub.
Harris and the boy do all the interesting work—the lugging and
the reefing, the letting her go and the heeling her over, and all
that sort of thing—leaving George and myself to do the peeling
of the potatoes and the washing up.

'Very well, then,' said Harris, 'let's take a proper yacht, with
a skipper, and do the thing in style.'

That also I objected to.   I know that skipper; his notion of
yachting is to lie in what he calls the 'offing,' where he can be
well in touch with his wife and family, to say nothing of his
favourite public-house.

Years ago, when I was young and inexperienced, I hired a
yacht myself.   Three things had combined to lead me into this
foolishness: I had had a stroke of unexpected luck; Ethelbertha
had expressed a yearning for sea air; and the very next morning,
in taking up casually at the club a copy of the *Sportsman*, I had
come across the following advertisement:

TO YACHTSMEN.—Unique Opportunity.—'Rogue,' 28-
ton Yawl.—Owner, called away suddenly on business, is
willing to let this superbly-fitted 'greyhound of the sea' for any
period short or long.   Two cabins and saloon; pianette, by
Woffenkoff; new copper.   Terms, 10 guineas a week.—Apply
Pertwee & Co., 3A Bucklersbury.

It had seemed to me like the answer to a prayer.   'The new
copper' did not interest me; what little washing we might want
could wait, I thought.   But the 'pianette by Woffenkoff'
sounded alluring.   I pictured Ethelbertha playing in the evening
—something with a chorus, in which, the crew, with a little
training, might join—while our moving home bounded, 'grey-
hound-like,' over the silvery billows.

I took a cab and drove direct to 3A Bucklersbury.   Mr Pertwee
was an unpretentious-looking gentleman, who had an unostenta-
tious office on the third floor.   He showed me a picture in water-
colours of the *Rogue* flying before the wind.   The deck was at an
angle of 95 to the ocean.   In the picture no human beings were
represented on the deck; I suppose they had slipped off.
Indeed, I do not see how anyone could have kept on, unless

nailed. I pointed out this disadvantage to the agent, who, however, explained to me that the picture represented the *Rogue* doubling something or other on the well-known occasion of her winning the Medway Challenge Shield. Mr Pertwee assumed that I knew all about the event, so that I did not like to ask any questions. Two specks near the frame of the picture, which at first I had taken for moths, represented, it appeared, the second and third winners in this celebrated race. A photograph of the yacht at anchor off Gravesend was less impressive, but suggested more stability. All answers to my inquiries being satisfactory, I took the thing for a fortnight. Mr Pertwee said it was fortunate I wanted it only for a fortnight—later on I came to agree with him—the time fitting in exactly with another hiring. Had I required it for three weeks he would have been compelled to refuse me.

The letting being thus arranged, Mr Pertwee asked me if I had a skipper in my eye. That I had not was also fortunate—things seemed to be turning out luckily for me all round—because Mr Pertwee felt sure I could not do better than keep on Mr Goyles, at present in charge—an excellent skipper, so Mr Pertwee assured me, a man who knew the sea as a man knows his own wife, and who had never lost a life.

It was still early in the day, and the yacht was lying off Harwich. I caught the ten forty-five from Liverpool Street, and by one o'clock was talking to Mr Goyles on deck. He was a stout man, and had a fatherly way with him. I told him my idea, which was to take the outlying Dutch islands and then creep up to Norway. He said, 'Aye aye, sir,' and appeared quite enthusiastic about the trip; said he should enjoy it himself. We came to the question of victualling, and he grew more enthusiastic. The amount of food suggested by Mr Goyles, I confess, surprised me. Had we been living in the days of Drake and the Spanish Main, I should have feared he was arranging for something illegal. However, he laughed in his fatherly way, and assured me we were not overdoing it. Anything left the crew would divide and take home with them—it seemed this was the custom. It appeared to me that I was providing for this crew for the winter, but I did not like to appear stingy, and said no more. The amount of drink required also surprised me. I arranged for what I thought we should need for ourselves, and then Mr Goyles spoke up for the crew. I must say that for him, he did think of his men.

'We don't want anything in the nature of an orgy, Mr Goyles,' I suggested.

'Orgy!' replied Mr Goyles; 'why they'll take that little drop in their tea.'

He explained to me that his motto was: 'Get good men and treat them well.'

'They work better for you,' said Mr Goyles; 'and they come again.'

Personally, I didn't feel I wanted them to come again. I was beginning to take a dislike to them before I had seen them; I regarded them as a greedy and guzzling crew. But Mr Goyles was so cheerfully emphatic, and I was so inexperienced, that again I let him have his way. He also promised that even in this department he would see to it personally that nothing was wasted.

I also left him to engage the crew. He said he could do the thing, and would, for me, with the help of two men and a boy. If he was alluding to the clearing up of the victuals and drink, I think he was making an underestimate; but possibly he may have been speaking of the sailing of the yacht.

I called at my tailors on the way home and ordered a yachting suit, with a white hat, which they promised to bustle up and have ready in time; and then I went home and told Ethelbertha all I had done. Her delight was clouded by only one reflection— would the dressmaker be able to finish a yachting costume for her in time? That is so like a woman.

Our honeymoon, which had taken place not very long before, had been somewhat curtailed, so we decided we would invite nobody, but have the yacht to ourselves. And thankful I am to heaven that we did so decide. On Monday we put on all our clothes and started. I forget what Ethelbertha wore, but, whatever it may have been, it looked very fetching. My own costume was a dark blue, trimmed with a narrow white braid, which, I think, was rather effective.

Mr Goyles met us on deck, and told us that lunch was ready. I must admit Goyles had secured the services of a very fair cook. The capabilities of the other members of the crew I had no opportunity of judging. Speaking of them in a state of rest, however, I can say of them they appeared to be a cheerful crew.

My idea had been that so soon as the men had finished their dinner we would weigh anchor, while I, smoking a cigar, with Ethelbertha by my side, would lean over the gunwale and watch the white cliffs of the Fatherland sink imperceptibly into the horizon. Ethelbertha and I carried out our part of the programme, and waited, with the deck to ourselves.

'They seem to be taking their time,' said Ethelbertha.

'If, in the course of fourteen days,' I said, 'they eat half of what is on this yacht, they will want a fairly long time for every meal. We had better not hurry them, or they won't get through a quarter of it.'

'They must have gone to sleep,' said Ethelbertha, later on. 'It will be tea-time soon.'

They were certainly very quiet. I went for'ard, and hailed Captain Goyles down the ladder. I hailed him three times; then he came up slowly. He appeared to be a heavier and older man than when I had seen him last. He had a cold cigar in his mouth.

'When you are ready, Captain Goyles,' I said, 'we'll start.'

Captain Goyles removed the cigar from his mouth.

'Not to-day we won't sir,' he replied, '*with* your permission.'

'Why, what's the matter with to-day?' I said. I know sailors are a superstitious folk; I thought maybe a Monday might be considered unlucky.

'The day's all right,' answered Captain Goyles, 'it's the wind I'm a-thinking of. It don't look much like changing.'

'But do we want it to change?' I asked. 'It seems to me to be just where it should be, dead behind us.'

'Aye aye,' said Captain Goyles, 'dead's the right word to use, for dead we'd all be, bar providence, if we was to put out in this. You see, sir,' he explained, in answer to my look of surprise, 'this is what we call a "land wind," that is, it's a-blowing, as one might say, direct off the land.'

When I came to think of it the man was right; the wind was blowing off the land.

'It may change in the night,' said Captain Goyles, more hopefully; 'anyhow, it's not violent, and she rides well.'

Captain Goyles resumed his cigar, and I returned aft, and explained to Ethelbertha the reason for the delay. Ethelbertha, who appeared to be less high spirited than when we first boarded, wanted to know *why* we couldn't sail when the wind was off the land.

'If it was not blowing off the land,' said Ethelbertha, 'it would be blowing off the sea, and that would send us back into the shore again. It seems to me this is just the very wind we want.'

I said: 'That is your inexperience, love; it *seems* to be the very wind we want, but it is not.   It's what we call a land wind, and a land wind is always very dangerous.'

Ethelbertha wanted to know *why* a land wind was very dangerous.

Her argumentativeness annoyed me somewhat; maybe I was feeling a bit cross; the monotonous rolling heave of a small yacht at anchor depresses an ardent spirit.

'I can't explain it to you,' I replied, which was true, 'but to set sail in this wind would be the height of foolhardiness, and I care for you too much, dear, to expose you to unnecessary risks.'

I thought this rather a neat conclusion, but Ethelbertha merely replied that she wished, under the circumstances, we hadn't come on board till Tuesday, and went below.

In the morning the wind veered round to the north; I was up early, and observed this to Captain Goyles.

'Aye aye, sir,' he remarked; 'it's unfortunate, but it can't be helped.'

'You don't think it possible for us to start to-day?' I hazarded.

He did not get angry with me, he only laughed.

'Well, sir,' said he, 'if you was a-wanting to go to Ipswich, I should say as it couldn't be better for us, but our destination being, as you see, the Dutch coast—why there you are!'

I broke the news to Ethelbertha, and we agreed to spend the day on shore.   Harwich is not a merry town, towards evening you might call it dull.   We had some tea and watercress at Dovercourt, and then returned to the quay to look for Captain Goyles and the boat.   We waited an hour for him.   When he came he was more cheerful than we were; if he had not told me himself that he never drank anything but one glass of hot grog before turning in for the night, I should have said he was drunk.

The next morning the wind was in the south, which made Captain Goyles rather anxious, it appearing that it was equally unsafe to move or to stop where we were; our only hope was it would change before anything happened.   By this time, Ethelbertha had taken a dislike to the yacht; she said that, personally, she would rather be spending a week in a bathing-machine, seeing that a bathing-machine was at least steady.

We passed another day in Harwich, and that night and the next, the wind still continuing in the south, we slept at the King's Head.   On Friday the wind was blowing direct from the east. I met Captain Goyles on the quay, and suggested that, under these circumstances, we might start. He appeared irritated at my persistence.

'If you knew a bit more, sir,' he said, 'you'd see for yourself that it's impossible. The wind's a-blowing direct off the sea.'

I said: 'Captain Goyles, tell me what is this thing I have hired? Is it a yacht or a house-boat?'

He seemed surprised at my question.

He said: 'It's a yawl.'

'What I mean is,' I said, 'can it be moved at all, or is it a fixture here? If it is a fixture,' I continued, 'tell me so frankly, then we will get some ivy in boxes and train over the port-holes, stick some flowers and an awning on deck, and make the thing look pretty. If, on the other hand, it can be moved——'

'Moved!' interrupted Captain Goyles. 'You get the right wind behind the *Rogue*——'

I said: 'What is the right wind?'

Captain Goyles looked puzzled.

'In the course of this week,' I went on, 'we have had wind from the north, from the south, from the east, from the west— with variations. If you can think of any other point of the compass from which it can blow, tell me, and I will wait for it. If not, and if that anchor has not grown into the bottom of the ocean, we will have it up to-day and see what happens.'

He grasped the fact that I was determined.

'Very well, sir,' he said, 'you're master and I'm man. I've only got one child as is still dependent on me, thank God, and no doubt your executors will feel it their duty to do the right thing by the old woman.'

His solemnity impressed me.

'Mr Goyles,' I said, 'be honest with me. Is there any hope, in any weather, of getting away from this damned hole?'

Captain Goyle's kindly geniality returned to him.

'You see, sir,' he said, 'this is a very peculiar coast. We'd be all right if we were once out, but getting away from it in a cockle-shell like that—well, to be frank, sir, it wants doing.'

I left Captain Goyles with the assurance that he would watch the weather as a mother would her sleeping babe; it was his own simile, and it struck me as rather touching. I saw him again at twelve o'clock; he was watching it from the window of the Chain and Anchor.

At five o'clock that evening a stroke of luck occurred; in the middle of the High Street I met a couple of yachting friends, who

Captain Goyles watching the weather

had had to put in by reason of a strained rudder. I told them my story, and they appeared less surprised than amused. Captain Goyles and the two men were still watching the weather. I ran into the King's Head, and prepared Ethelbertha. The four of us crept quietly down to the quay, where we found our boat. Only the boy was on board; my two friends took charge of the yacht, and by six o'clock we were scudding merrily up the coast.

We put in that night at Aldborough, and the next day worked up to Yarmouth, where, as my friends had to leave, I decided to abandon the yacht. We sold the stores by auction on Yarmouth sands early in the morning. I made a loss, but had the satisfaction of 'doing' Captain Goyles. I left the *Rogue* in charge of a local mariner, who, for a couple of sovereigns, undertook to see to its return to Harwich; and we came back to London by train. There may be yachts other than the *Rogue*, and skippers other than Mr Goyles, but that experience has prejudiced me against both.

George also thought a yacht would be a good deal of responsibility, so we dismissed the idea.

'What about the river?' suggested Harris. 'We have had some pleasant times on that.'

George pulled in silence at his cigar, and I cracked another nut.

'The river is not what it used to be,' said I; 'I don't know what, but there's a something—a dampness—about the river air that always starts my lumbago.'

'It's the same with me,' said George. 'I don't know how it is, but I never can sleep now in the neighbourhood of the river. I spent a week at Joe's place in the spring, and every night I woke up at seven o'clock and never got a wink afterwards.'

'I merely suggested it,' observed Harris. 'Personally, I don't think it good for me, either; it touches my gout.'

'What suits me best,' I said, 'is mountain air. What say you to a walking tour in Scotland?'

'It's always wet in Scotland,' said George. 'I was three weeks in Scotland the year before last, and was never dry once all the time—not in that sense.'

'It's fine enough in Switzerland,' said Harris.

'They would never stand our going to Switzerland by ourselves,' I objected. 'You know what happened last time. It must be some place where no delicately nurtured woman or child could possibly live; a country of bad hotels and comfortless

travelling; where we shall have to rough it, to work hard, to
starve perhaps——'

'Easy!' interrupted George, 'easy, there! Don't forget I'm
coming with you.'

'It's always wet in Scotland'

'I have it!' exclaimed Harris; 'a bicycle tour!'

George looked doubtful.

'There's a lot of uphill about a bicycle tour,' said he, 'and the
wind is against you.'

'So there is downhill, and the wind behind you,' said Harris.

'I've never noticed it,' said George.

'You won't think of anything better than a bicycle tour,' persisted Harris.

I was inclined to agree with him.

'And I'll tell you where,' continued he: 'through the Black Forest.'

'Why, that's *all* uphill,' said George.

'Not all,' retorted Harris; 'say two-thirds. And there's one thing you've forgotten.'

He looked round cautiously and sunk his voice to a whisper.

'There are little railways going up those hills, little cogwheel things that——'

The door opened, and Mrs Harris appeared. She said that Ethelbertha was putting on her bonnet, and that Muriel, after waiting, had given 'The Mad Hatter's Tea Party' without us.

'Club, to-morrow, at four,' whispered Harris to me, as he rose, and I passed it on to George as we went upstairs.

CHAPTER II

I OPENED the ball with Ethelbertha that same evening. I commenced by being purposely a little irritable. My idea was that Ethelbertha would remark upon this. I should admit it, and account for it by over brain pressure. This would naturally lead to talk about my health in general, and the evident necessity there was for my taking prompt and vigorous measures. I thought that with a little tact I might even manage so that the suggestion should come from Ethelbertha herself. I imagined her saying: 'No, dear, it is change you want; complete change. Now, be persuaded by me, and go away for a month. No, do not ask me to come with you. I know you would rather that I did, but I will not. It is the society of other men you need. Try and persuade George and Harris to go with you. Believe me, a highly strung brain such as yours demands occasional relaxation from the strain of domestic surroundings. Forget for a little while that children want music lessons, and boots, and bicycles, with tincture of rhubarb three times a day; forget there are such things in life as cooks, and house decorators, and next-door dogs, and butchers' bills. Go away to some green corner of the earth, where all is new and strange to you, where your overwrought mind will gather peace and fresh ideas. Go away for a space and give me time to miss you, and to reflect upon your goodness and virtue, which, continually present with me, I may, human-like, be apt to forget, as one, through use, grows indifferent to the blessing of the sun and the beauty of the moon. Go away, and come back refreshed in mind and body, a brighter, better man—if that be possible—than when you went away.'

But even when we obtain our desires they never come to us garbed as we would wish. To begin with, Ethelbertha did not seem to remark that I was irritable; I had to draw her attention to it. I said:

'You must forgive me, I'm not feeling quite myself to-night.'

She said: 'Oh! I have not noticed anything different; what's the matter with you?'

'I can't tell you what it is,' I said; 'I've felt it coming on for weeks.'

'It's that whisky,' said Ethelbertha. 'You never touch it except when we go to the Harris's. You know you can't stand it; you have not a strong head.'

'It isn't the whisky,' I replied; 'it's deeper than that. I fancy it's more mental than bodily.'

'You've been reading those criticisms again,' said Ethelbertha, more sympathetically; 'why don't you take my advice and put them on the fire?'

'And it isn't the criticisms,' I answered; 'they've been quite flattering of late—one or two of them.'

'Well, what is it?' said Ethelbertha. 'There must be something to account for it.'

'No, there isn't,' I replied; 'that's the remarkable thing about it; I can only describe it as a strange feeling of unrest that seems to have taken possession of me.'

Ethelbertha glanced across at me with a somewhat curious expression, I thought; but as she said nothing, I continued the argument myself.

'This aching monotony of life, these days of peaceful, uneventful felicity, they appal one.'

'I should not grumble at them,' said Ethelbertha, 'we might get some of the other sort, and like them still less.'

'I'm not so sure of that,' I replied. 'In a life of continuous joy, I can imagine even pain coming as a welcome variation. I wonder sometimes whether the saints in heaven do not occasionally feel the continual serenity a burden. To myself, a life of endless bliss, uninterrupted by a single contrasting note, would, I feel, grow maddening. I suppose,' I continued, 'I am a strange sort of man; I can hardly understand myself at times. There are moments,' I added, 'when I hate myself.'

Often a little speech like this, hinting at hidden depths of indescribable emotion, has touched Ethelbertha, but to-night she appeared strangely unsympathetic. With regard to heaven and its possible effect upon me, she suggested my not worrying myself about that, remarking it was always foolish to go half-way to meet trouble that might never come; while as to my being a strange sort of fellow, that, she supposed, I could not help, and if other people were willing to put up with me, there was an end of the matter. The monotony of life, she added, was a common experience; there she could sympathize with me.

'You don't know how I long,' said Ethelbertha, 'to get away occasionally, even from you; but I know it can never be, so I do not brood upon it.'

I had never heard Ethelbertha speak like this before; it astonished and grieved me beyond measure.

'That's not a very kind remark to make,' I said, 'not a wifely remark.'

'I know it isn't,' she replied; 'that is why I have never said it before. You men never can understand,' continued Ethelbertha, 'that, however fond a woman may be of a man, there are times when he palls upon her. You don't know how I long to be able sometimes to put on my bonnet and go out, with nobody to ask me where I am going, why I am going, how long I am going to be, and when I shall be back. You don't know how I sometimes long to order a dinner that I should like, and that the children would like, but at the sight of which you would put on your hat and be off to the Club. You don't know how much I feel inclined sometimes to invite some woman here that I like, and that I know you don't; to go and see the people that *I* want to see, to go to bed when *I* am tired, and to get up when *I* feel I want to get up. Two people living together are bound both to be continually sacrificing their own desires to the other one. It is sometimes a good thing to slacken the strain a bit.'

On thinking over Ethelbertha's words afterwards, I have come to see their wisdom; but at the time I admit I was hurt and indignant.

'If your desire,' I said, 'is to get rid of me——'

'Now, don't be an old goose,' said Ethelbertha; 'I only want to get rid of you for a little while, just long enough to forget there are one or two corners about you that are not perfect, just long enough to let me remember what a dear fellow you are in other respects, and to look forward to your return, as I used to look forward to your coming in the old days when I did not see you so often as to become, perhaps, a little indifferent to you, as one grows indifferent to the glory of the sun, just because he is there every day.'

I did not like the tone that Ethelbertha took. There seemed

to be a frivolity about her, unsuited to the theme into which we had drifted. That a woman should contemplate cheerfully an absence of three or four weeks from her husband appeared to me to be not altogether nice, not what I call womanly; it was not like Ethelbertha at all. I was worried, I felt I didn't want to go this trip at all. If it had not been for George and Harris, I would have abandoned it. As it was, I could not see how to change my mind with dignity.

'Very well, Ethelbertha,' I replied, 'it shall be as you wish. If you desire a holiday from my presence, you shall enjoy it; but if it be not impertinent curiosity on the part of a husband, I should like to know what you propose doing in my absence?'

'We will take that house at Folkestone,' answered Ethelbertha, 'and I'll go down there with Kate. And if you want to do Clara Harris a good turn,' added Ethelbertha, 'you'll persuade Harris to go with you, and then Clara can join us. We three used to have some very jolly times together before you men ever came along, and it would be just delightful to renew them. Do you think,' continued Ethelbertha, 'that you could persuade Mr Harris to go with you?'

I said I would try.

'There's a dear boy,' said Ethelbertha; 'try hard. You might get George to join you.'

I replied there was not much advantage in George's coming, seeing he was a bachelor, and that therefore nobody would be much benefited by his absence. But a woman never understands satire. Ethelbertha merely remarked it would look unkind leaving him behind. I promised to put it to him.

I met Harris at the Club in the afternoon, and asked him how he had got on.

He said: 'Oh, that's all right; there's no difficulty about getting away.'

But there was that about his tone that suggested incomplete satisfaction, so I pressed him for further details.

'She was as sweet as milk about it,' he continued; 'said it was an excellent idea of George's, and that she thought it would do me good.'

'That seems all right,' I said; 'what's wrong about that?'

'There's nothing wrong about that,' he answered, 'but that wasn't all. She went on to talk of other things.'

'I understand,' I said.

'There's that bath-room fad of hers,' he continued.

'I've heard of it,' I said, 'she has started Ethelbertha on the same idea.'

'Well, I've had to agree to that being put in hand at once; I couldn't argue any more when she was so nice about the other thing.   That will cost me a hundred pounds, at the very least.'

'As much as that?' I asked.

'Every penny of it,' said Harris; 'the estimate alone is sixty.' I was sorry to hear him say this.

'Then there's the kitchen stove,' continued Harris; 'everything that has gone wrong in the house for the last two years has been the fault of that kitchen stove.'

'I know,' I said.   'We have been in seven houses since we were married, and every kitchen stove has been worse than the last.   Our present one is not only incompetent; it is spiteful.   It knows when we are giving a party, and goes out of its way to do its worst.'

'*We* are going to have a new one,' said Harris, but he did not say it proudly.   'Clara thought it would be such a saving of expense, having the two things done at the same time.   I believe,' said Harris, 'if a woman wanted a diamond tiara, she would explain that it was to save the expense of a bonnet.'

'How much do you reckon the stove is going to cost you?' I asked.   I felt interested in the subject.

'I don't know,' answered Harris; 'another twenty, I suppose. Then we talked about the piano.   Could you ever notice,' said Harris, 'any difference between one piano and another?'

'Some of them seem to be a bit louder than others,' I answered; 'but one gets used to that.'

'Ours is all wrong about the treble,' said Harris.   'By the way, what *is* the treble?'

'It's the shrill end of the thing,' I explained; 'the part that sounds as if you'd trod on its tail.   The brilliant selections always end up with a flourish on it.'

'They want more of it,' said Harris; 'our old one hasn't got enough of it.   I'll have to put it in the nursery, and get a new one for the drawing-room.'

'Anything else?' I asked.

'No,' said Harris; 'she didn't seem able to think of anything else.'

'You'll find when you get home,' I said, 'she has thought of one other thing.'

'What's that?' said Harris.

'A house at Folkestone for the season.'

'What should she want a house at Folkestone for?' said Harris.

'To live in,' I suggested, 'during the summer months.'

'She's going to her people in Wales,' said Harris, 'for the holidays, with the children; we've had an invitation.'

'Possibly,' I said, 'she'll go to Wales before she goes to Folkestone, or maybe she'll take Wales on her way home; but she'll want a house at Folkestone for the season, notwithstanding. I may be mistaken—I hope for your sake that I am—but I feel a presentiment that I'm not.'

'This trip,' said Harris, 'is going to be expensive.'

'It was an idiotic suggestion,' I said, 'from the beginning.'

'It was foolish of us to listen to him,' said Harris; 'he'll get us into real trouble one of these days.'

'He always was a muddler,' I agreed.

'So headstrong,' added Harris.

We heard his voice at that moment in the hall, asking for letters.

'Better not say anything to him,' I suggested; 'it's too late to go back now.'

'There would be no advantage in doing so,' replied Harris. 'I should have to get that bath-room and piano in any case now.'

He came in looking very cheerful.

'Well,' he said, 'is it all right? Have you managed it?'

There was that about his tone I did not altogether like; I noticed Harris resented it also.

'Managed what?' I said.

'Why, to get off,' said George.

I felt the time was come to explain things to George.

'In married life,' I said, 'the man proposes, the woman submits. It is her duty; all religion teaches it.'

George folded his hands and fixed his eyes on the ceiling.

'We may chaff and joke a little about these things,' I continued; 'but when it comes to practice, that is what always happens. We have mentioned to our wives that we are going. Naturally, they are grieved; they would prefer to come with us; failing that, they would have us remain with them. But we have explained to them our wishes on the subject, and—there's an end of the matter.'

George said: 'Forgive me; I did not understand. I am only a bachelor. People tell me this, that, and the other, and I listen.'

I said: 'That is where you do wrong. When you want information come to Harris or myself; we will tell you the truth about these questions.'

George thanked us, and we proceeded with the business in hand.

'When shall we start?' said George.

'So far as I am concerned,' replied Harris, 'the sooner the better.'

His idea, I fancy, was to get away before Mrs H. thought of other things. We fixed the following Wednesday.

'What about route?' said Harris.

'I have an idea,' said George. 'I take it you fellows are naturally anxious to improve your minds?'

I said: 'We don't want to become monstrosities. To a reasonable degree, yes, if it can be done without much expense and with little personal trouble.'

'It can,' said George. 'We know Holland and the Rhine. Very well, my suggestion is that we take the boat to Hamburg, see Berlin and Dresden, and work our way to the Schwarzwald, through Nuremburg and Stuttgart.'

'There are some pretty bits in Mesopotamia, so I've been told,' murmured Harris.

George said Mesopotamia was too much out of our way, but that the Berlin–Dresden route was quite practicable. For good or evil, he persuaded us into it.

'The machines, I suppose,' said George, 'as before. Harris and I on the tandem, J.——'

'I think not,' interrupted Harris firmly. 'You and J. on the tandem, I on the single.'

'All the same to me,' agreed George. 'J. and I on the tandem, Harris——'

'I do not mind taking my turn,' I interrupted, 'but I am not going to carry George *all* the way; the burden should be divided.'

'Very well,' agreed Harris, 'we'll divide it. But it must be on the distinct understanding that he works.'

'That he what?' said George.

'That he works,' repeated Harris firmly; 'at all events, uphill.'

'Great Scott!' said George; 'don't you want *any* exercise?'

There is always unpleasantness about this tandem. It is the theory of the man in front that the man behind does nothing; it is equally the theory of the man behind that he alone is the motive power, the man in front merely doing the puffing. The mystery will never be solved. It is annoying when Prudence is whispering to you on the one side not to overdo your strength and bring on heart disease; while Justice into the other ear is remarking: 'Why should you do it all? This isn't a cab. He's not your passenger': to hear him grunt out:

'What's the matter—lost your pedals?'

Harris, in his early married days, made much trouble for himself on one occasion, owing to this impossibility of knowing what the person behind is doing. He was riding with his wife through Holland. The roads were stony, and the machine jumped a good deal.

'Sit tight,' said Harris, without turning his head.

What Mrs Harris thought he said was, 'Jump off.' Why she should have thought he said 'Jump off,' when he said 'Sit tight,' neither of them can explain.

Mrs Harris puts it in this way: 'If you had said, "Sit tight," why should I have jumped off?'

Harris puts it: 'If I had wanted you to jump off, why should I have said "Sit tight"?'

The bitterness is past, but they argue about the matter to this day.

Be the explanation what it may, however, nothing alters the fact that Mrs Harris did jump off, while Harris pedalled away hard, under the impression she was still behind him. It appears that at first she thought he was riding up the hill merely to show off. They were both young in those days, and he used to do that sort of thing. She expected him to spring to earth on reaching the summit, and lean in a careless and graceful attitude against the machine, waiting for her. When, on the contrary, she saw him pass the summit and proceed rapidly down a long and steep incline, she was seized, first with surprise, secondly with indignation, and lastly with alarm. She ran to the top of the hill and shouted, but he never turned his head. She watched him disappear into a wood a mile and a half distant, and then sat down and cried. They had had a slight difference that morning, and she wondered if he had taken it seriously and intended desertion. She had no money; she knew no Dutch. People passed, and seemed sorry for her; she tried to make them understand what had happened. They gathered that she had lost something, but could not grasp what. They took her to the nearest village, and found a policeman for her. He concluded from her pantomime that some man had stolen her bicycle. They put the telegraph

into operation, and discovered in a village four miles off an
unfortunate boy riding a lady's machine of an obsolete pattern.
They brought him to her in a cart, but as she did not appear to
want either him or his bicycle they let him go again, and resigned
themselves to bewilderment.

Meanwhile Harris continued his ride with much enjoyment.
It seemed to him that he had suddenly become a stronger, and in
every way a more capable cyclist.   Said he to what he thought
was Mrs Harris:

'I haven't felt this machine so light for months.   It's this air,
I think; it's doing me good.'

Then he told her not to be afraid, and he would show her how
fast he *could* go.   He bent down over the handles, and put his
heart into his work.   The bicycle bounded over the road like a
thing of life; farmhouses and churches, dogs and chickens came
to him and passed.   Old folks stood and gazed at him, the
children cheered him.

In this way he sped merrily onward for about five miles.
Then, as he explains it, the feeling began to grow upon him that
something was wrong.   He was not surprised at the silence; the
wind was blowing strongly, and the machine was rattling a good
deal.   It was a sense of void that came upon him.   He stretched
out his hand behind him, and felt; there was nothing there but
space.   He jumped, or rather fell off, and looked back up the
road; it stretched white and straight through the dark wood, and
not a living soul could be seen upon it.   He remounted, and rode
back up the hill.   In ten minutes he came to where the road
broke into four; there he dismounted and tried to remember
which fork he had come down.

While he was deliberating, a man passed, sitting sideways on a
horse.   Harris stopped him, and explained to him that he had
lost his wife.   The man appeared to be neither surprised nor
sorry for him.   While they were talking another farmer came
along, to whom the first man explained the matter, not as an
accident, but as a good story.   What appeared to surprise the
second man most was that Harris should be making a fuss about
the thing.   He could get no sense out of either of them, and
cursing them he mounted his machine again, and took the middle
road on chance.   Half-way up, he came upon a party of two
young women with one young man between them.   They
appeared to be making the most of him.   He asked them if they
had seen his wife.   They asked him what she was like.   He did

not know enough Dutch to describe her properly; all he could tell them was she was a very beautiful woman, of medium size. Evidently this did not satisfy them, the description was too general; any man could say that, and by this means perhaps get possession of a wife that did not belong to him. They asked him how she was dressed; for the life of him he could not recollect.

I doubt if any man could tell how any woman was dressed ten minutes after he had left her. He recollected a blue skirt, and then there was something that carried the dress on, as it were, up to the neck. Possibly, this may have been a blouse; he retained a dim vision of a belt; but what sort of a blouse? Was it green, or yellow, or blue? Had it a collar, or was it fastened with a bow? Were there feathers in her hat, or flowers? Or was it a hat at all? He dared not say, for fear of making a mistake and being sent miles after the wrong party. The two young women giggled, which in his then state of mind irritated Harris. The young man, who appeared anxious to get rid of him, suggested the police station at the next town. Harris made his way there. The police gave him a piece of paper, and told him to write down a full description of his wife, together with details of when and where he had lost her. He did not know where he had lost her; all he could tell them was the name of the village where he had lunched. He knew he had her with him then, and that they had started from there together.

The police looked suspicious; they were doubtful about three matters: Firstly, was she really his wife? Secondly, had he really lost her? Thirdly, why had he lost her? With the aid of a hotel-keeper, however, who spoke a little English, he overcame their scruples. They promised to act, and in the evening they brought her to him in a covered wagon, together with a bill for expenses. The meeting was not a tender one. Mrs Harris is not a good actress, and always has great difficulty in disguising her feelings. On this occasion, she frankly admits, she made no attempt to disguise them.

The wheel business settled, there arose the everlasting luggage question.

'The usual list, I suppose,' said George, preparing to write.

That was wisdom I had taught them; I had learned it myself years ago from my Uncle Podger.

'Always, before beginning to pack,' my uncle would say, 'make a list.'

He was a methodical man.

'Take a piece of paper'—he always began at the beginning—
'put down on it everything you can possibly require; then go
over it and see that it contains nothing you can possibly do
without. Imagine yourself in bed; what have you got on?
Very well, put it down—together with a change. You get up;
what do you do? Wash yourself. What do you wash yourself
with? Soap; put down soap. Go on till you have finished.
Then take your clothes. Begin at your feet; what do you wear
on your feet? Boots, shoes, socks; put them down. Work up
till you get to your head. What else do you want besides
clothes? A little brandy; put it down. A corkscrew; put it
down. Put down everything, then you don't forget anything.'

That is the plan he always pursued himself. The list made,
he would go over it carefully, as he always advised to see that he
had forgotten nothing. Then he would go over it again, and
strike out everything it was possible to dispense with.

Then he would lose the list.

Said George: 'Just sufficient for a day or two we will take with
us on our bikes. The bulk of our luggage we must send on from
town to town.'

'We must be careful,' I said; 'I knew a man once——'

Harris looked at his watch.

'We'll hear about him on the boat,' said Harris; 'I have got
to meet Clara at Waterloo Station in half an hour.'

'It won't take half an hour,' I said; 'it's a true story, and——'

'Don't waste it,' said George: 'I am told there are rainy
evenings in the Black Forest; we may be glad of it. What we
have to do now is to finish this list.'

Now I come to think of it, I never did get off that story; something always interrupted it. And it really was true.

CHAPTER III

ON Monday afternoon Harris came round; he had a cycling paper in his hand.

I said: 'If you take my advice, you will leave it alone.'

Harris said: 'Leave what alone?'

I said: 'That brand-new, patent, revolution in cycling, record-breaking, tomfoolishness, whatever it may be, the advertisement of which you have there in your hand.'

He said: 'Well, I don't know; there will be some steep hills for us to negotiate; I guess we shall want a good brake.'

I said: 'We shall want a brake, I agree; what we shall not want is a mechanical surprise that we don't understand, and that never acts when it is wanted.'

'This thing,' he said, 'acts automatically.'

'You needn't tell me,' I said. 'I know exactly what it will do, by instinct. Going uphill it will jamb the wheel so effectively that we shall have to carry the machine bodily. The air at the top of the hill will do it good, and it will suddenly come right again. Going downhill it will start reflecting what a nuisance it has been. This will lead to remorse, and finally to despair. It will say to itself: "I'm not fit to be a brake. I don't help these fellows; I only hinder them. I'm a curse, that's what I am"; and, without a word of warning, it will "chuck" the whole business. That is what that brake will do. Leave it alone. You are a good fellow,' I continued, 'but you have one fault.'

'What?' he asked indignantly.

'You have too much faith,' I answered. 'If you read an advertisement, you go away and believe it. Every experiment that every fool has thought of in connection with cycling you have tried. Your guardian angel appears to be a capable and

25

conscientious spirit, and hitherto she has seen you through; take my advice and don't try her too far. She must have had a busy time since you started cycling. Don't go on till you make her mad.'

He said: 'If every man talked like that there would be no advancement made in any department of life. If nobody ever tried a new thing the world would come to a standstill. It is by——'

'I know all that can be said on that side of the argument,' I interrupted. 'I agree in trying new experiments up to thirty-five; *after* thirty-five I consider a man is entitled to think of himself. You and I have done our duty in this direction, you especially. You have been blown up by a patent gas lamp——'

He said: 'I really think, you know, that was my fault; I think I must have screwed it up too tight.'

I said: 'I am quite willing to believe that if there was a wrong way of handling the thing that is the way you handle it. You should take that tendency of yours into consideration; it bears upon the argument. Myself, I did not notice what you did; I only know we were riding peacefully and pleasantly along the Whitby Road, discussing the Thirty Years War, when your lamp went off like a pistol shot. The start sent me into the ditch; and your wife's face, when I told her there was nothing the matter and that she was not to worry, because the two men would carry you upstairs, and the doctor would be round in a minute bringing the nurse with him, still lingers in my memory.'

He said: 'I wish you had thought to pick up the lamp. I should like to have found out what was the cause of its going off like that.'

I said: 'There was not time to pick up the lamp. I calculate it would have taken two hours to have collected it. As to its "going off," the mere fact of its being advertised as the safest lamp ever invented would of itself, to anyone but you, have suggested accident. Then there was that electric lamp,' I continued.

'Well, that really did give a fine light,' he replied; 'you said so yourself.'

I said: 'It gave a brilliant light in the King's Road, Brighton, and frightened a horse. The moment we got into the dark beyond Kemp Town it went out, and you were summoned for riding without a light. You may remember that on sunny afternoons you used to ride about with that lamp shining for all it was

worth.   When lighting-up time came it was naturally tired, and
wanted a rest.'

'It was a bit irritating, that lamp,' he murmured; 'I remember it.'

I said: 'It irritated me; it must have been worse for you.
Then, there are saddles,' I went on—I wished to get this lesson

Ye frightened horse

home to him.   'Can you think of any saddle ever advertised that
you have *not* tried?'

He said: 'It has been an idea of mine that the right saddle is
to be found.'

I said: 'You give up that idea; this is an imperfect world of joy
and sorrow mingled.   There may be a better land where bicycle
saddles are made out of rainbow, stuffed with cloud; in this world
the simplest thing is to get used to something hard.   There was

that saddle you bought in Birmingham; it was divided in the middle, and looked like a pair of kidneys.'

He said: 'You mean that one constructed on anatomical principles.'

'Very likely,' I replied. 'The box you bought it in had a picture on the cover, representing a sitting skeleton—or rather that part of a skeleton which does sit.'

He said: 'It was quite correct; it showed you the true position of the——'

I said: 'We will not go into details; the picture always seemed to me indelicate.'

He said: 'Medically speaking, it was right.'

'Possibly,' I said, 'for a man who rode in nothing but his bones. I only know that I tried it myself, and that to a man who wore flesh it was agony. Every time you went over a stone or a rut it nipped you; it was like riding on an irritable lobster. You rode that for a month.'

'I thought it only right to give it a fair trial,' he answered.

I said: 'You gave your family a fair trial also; if you will allow me the use of slang. Your wife told me that never in the whole course of your married life had she known you so bad tempered, so unchristian-like, as you were that month. Then you remember that other saddle, the one with the spring under it.'

He said: 'You mean "the Spiral."'

I said: 'I mean the one that jerked you up and down like a jack-in-the-box; sometimes you came down again in the right place, and sometimes you didn't. I am not referring to these matters merely to recall painful memories, but I want to impress you with the folly of trying experiments at your time of life.'

He said: 'I wish you wouldn't harp so much on my age. A man at thirty-four——'

'A man at what?'

He said: 'If you don't want the thing, don't have it. If your machine runs away with you down a mountain, and you and George get flung through a church roof, don't blame me.'

'I cannot promise for George,' I said; 'a little thing will sometimes irritate him, as you know. If such an accident as you suggest happen, he may be cross, but I will undertake to explain to him that it was not your fault.'

'Is the thing all right?' he asked.

'The tandem,' I replied, 'is well.'

He said: 'Have you overhauled it?'

I said: 'I have not, nor is anyone else going to overhaul it. The thing is now in working order, and it is going to remain in working order till we start.'

I have had experience of this 'overhauling.' There was a man at Folkestone; I used to meet him on the Lees. He proposed one evening we should go for a long bicycle ride together on the following day, and I agreed. I got up early, for me; I made an effort, and was pleased with myself. He came half an hour late: I was waiting for him in the garden. It was a lovely day. He said:

'That's a good-looking machine of yours. How does it run?'

'Oh, like most of them!' I answered; 'easily enough in the morning; goes a little stiffly after lunch.'

He caught hold of it by the front wheel and the fork, and shook it violently.

I said: 'Don't do that; you'll hurt it.'

I did not see why he should shake it; it had not done anything to him. Besides, if it wanted shaking, I was the proper person to shake it. I felt much as I should had he started whacking my dog.

He said: 'This front wheel wobbles.'

I said: 'It doesn't if you don't wobble it.' It didn't wobble, as a matter of fact—nothing worth calling a wobble.

He said: 'This is dangerous; have you got a screw-hammer?'

I ought to have been firm, but I thought that perhaps he really did know something about the business. I wer to the tool shed to see what I could find. When I came back he was sitting on the ground with the front wheel between his legs. He was playing with it, twiddling it round between his fingers; the remnant of the machine was lying on the gravel path beside him.

He said: 'Something has happened to this front wheel of yours.'

'It looks like it, doesn't it?' I answered. But he was the sort of man that never understands satire.

He said: 'It looks to me as if the bearings were all wrong.'

I said: 'Don't you trouble about it any more; you will make yourself tired. Let us put it back and get off.'

He said: 'We may as well see what is the matter with it, now it is out.' He talked as though it had dropped out by accident.

Before I could stop him he had unscrewed something somewhere, and out rolled all over the path some dozen or so little balls.

The overhauling fiend

'Catch 'em!' he shouted; 'catch 'em! We mustn't lose any of them.' He was quite excited about them.

We grovelled round for half an hour, and found sixteen. He said he hoped we had got them all, because, if not, it would make a serious difference to the machine. He said there was nothing you should be more careful about in taking a bicycle to pieces than seeing you did not lose any of the balls. He explained that you ought to count them as you took them out, and see that exactly the same number went back in each place. I promised, if ever I took a bicycle to pieces I would remember his advice.

I put the balls for safety in my hat, and I put my hat upon the doorstep. It was not a sensible thing to do, I admit. As a matter of fact, it was a silly thing to do. I am not as a rule addle-headed; his influence must have affected me.

He then said that while he was about it he would see to the chain for me, and at once began taking off the gear-case. I did try to persuade him from that. I told him what an experienced friend of mine once said to me solemnly:

'If anything goes wrong with your gear-case, sell the machine and buy a new one; it comes cheaper.'

He said: 'People talk like that who understand nothing about machines. Nothing is easier than taking off a gear-case.'

I had to confess he was right. In less than five minutes he had the gear-case in two pieces, lying on the path, and was grovelling for screws. He said it was always a mystery to him the way screws disappeared.

We were still looking for the screws when Ethelbertha came out. She seemed surprised to find us there; she said she thought we had started hours ago.

He said: 'We shan't be long now. I'm just helping your husband to overhaul this machine of his. It's a good machine; but they all want going over occasionally.'

Ethelbertha said: 'If you want to wash yourselves when you have done you might go into the back kitchen, if you don't mind; the girls have just finished the bedrooms.'

She told me that if she met Kate they would probably go for a sail; but that in any case she would be back to lunch. I would have given a sovereign to be going with her. I was getting heartily sick of standing about watching this fool breaking up my bicycle.

Common sense continued to whisper to me: 'Stop him, before

he does any more mischief. You have a right to protect your own property from the ravages of a lunatic. Take him by the scruff of the neck, and kick him out of the gate!'

But I am weak when it comes to hurting other people's feelings, and I let him muddle on.

He gave up looking for the rest of the screws. He said screws had a knack of turning up when you least expected them, and that now he would see to the chain. He tightened it till it would not move; next he loosened it until it was twice as loose as it was before. Then he said we had better think about getting the front wheel back into its place again.

I held the fork open, and he worried with the wheel. At the end of ten minutes I suggested he should hold the forks, and that I should handle the wheel; and we changed places. At the end of his first minute he dropped the machine, and took a short walk round the croquet lawn, with his hands pressed together between his thighs. He explained as he walked that the thing to be careful about was to avoid getting your fingers pinched between the forks and the spokes of the wheel. I replied I was convinced, from my own experience, that there was much truth in what he said. He wrapped himself up in a couple of dusters, and we commenced again. At length we did get the thing into position; and the moment it was in position he burst out laughing.

I said: 'What's the joke?'

He said: 'Well, I am an ass!'

It was the first thing he had said that made me respect him. I asked him what had led him to the discovery.

He said: 'We've forgotten the balls!'

I looked for my hat; it was lying topsyturvy in the middle of the path, and Ethelbertha's favourite hound was swallowing the balls as fast as he could pick them up.

'He will kill himself,' said Ebbson—I have never met him since that day, thank the Lord; but I think his name was Ebbson—'they are solid steel.'

I said: 'I am not troubling about the dog. He has had a boot-lace and a packet of needles already this week. Nature's the best guide; puppies seem to require this kind of stimulant. What I am thinking about is my bicycle.'

He was of a cheerful disposition. He said: 'Well, we must put back all we can find, and trust to providence.'

We found eleven. We fixed six on one side and five on the

other, and half an hour later the wheel was in its place again. It need hardly be added that it really did wobble now; a child might have noticed it. Ebbson said it would do for the present. He appeared to be getting a bit tired himself. If I had let him, he would, I believe, at this point have gone home. I was determined now, however, that he should stop and finish; I had abandoned all thoughts of a ride. My pride in the machine he had killed. My only interest lay now in seeing him scratch and bump and pinch himself. I revived his drooping spirits with a glass of beer and some judicious praise. I said:

'Watching you do this is of real use to me. It is not only your skill and dexterity that fascinates me, it is your cheery confidence in yourself, your inexplicable hopefulness, that does me good.'

Thus encouraged, he set to work to refix the gear-case. He stood the bicycle against the house, and worked from the off side. Then he stood it against a tree, and worked from the near side. Then I held it for him, while he lay on the ground with his head between the wheels, and worked at it from below, and dropped oil upon himself. Then he took it away from me, and doubled himself across it like a pack-saddle, till he lost his balance and slid over on to his head. Three times he said:

'Thank heaven, that's right at last!'

And twice he said:

'No, I'm damned if it is after all!'

What he said the third time I try to forget.

Then he lost his temper and tried bullying the thing. The bicycle, I was glad to see, showed spirit; and the subsequent proceedings degenerated into little else than a rough-and-tumble fight between him and the machine. One moment the bicycle would be on the gravel path, and he on top of it; the next, the position would be reversed—he on the gravel path, the bicycle on him. Now he would be standing flushed with victory, the bicycle firmly fixed between his legs. But his triumph would be short-lived. By a sudden, quick movement it would free itself, and, turning upon him, hit him sharply over the head with one of its handles.

At a quarter to one, dirty and dishevelled, cut and bleeding, he said: 'I think that will do'; and rose and wiped his brow.

The bicycle looked as if it also had had enough of it. Which had received most punishment it would have been difficult to say. I took him into the back kitchen, where, so far as was possible without soda and proper tools, he cleaned himself, and sent him home.

The bicycle I put into a cab and took round to the nearest repairing shop. The foreman of the works came up and looked at it.

'What do you want me to do with that?' said he.

'I want you,' I said, 'so far as is possible, to restore it.'

'It's a bit far gone,' said he; 'but I'll do my best.'

He did his best, which came to two pounds ten. But it was never the same machine again; and at the end of the season I left it in an agent's hands to sell. I wished to deceive nobody; I instructed the man to advertise it as a last year's machine. The agent advised me not to mention any date. He said:

'In this business it isn't a question of what is true and what isn't; it's a question of what you can get people to believe. Now, between you and me, it don't look like a last year's machine; so far as looks are concerned, it might be a ten-year-old. We'll say nothing about date; we'll just get what we can.'

I left the matter to him, and he got me five pounds, which he said was more than he had expected.

There are two ways you can get exercise out of a bicycle: you can 'overhaul' it, or you can ride it. On the whole, I am not sure that a man who takes his pleasure overhauling does not have the best of the bargain. He is independent of the weather and the wind; the state of the roads troubles him not. Give him a screw-hammer, a bundle of rags, an oil-can, and something to sit down upon, and he is happy for the day. He has to put up with certain disadvantages, of course; there is no joy without alloy. He himself always looks like a tinker, and his machine always suggests the idea that, having stolen it, he has tried to disguise it; but as he rarely gets beyond the first milestone with it, this, perhaps, does not much matter. The mistake some people make is in thinking they can get both forms of sport out of the same machine. This is impossible; no machine will stand the double strain. You must make up your mind whether you are going to be an 'overhauler' or a rider. Personally, I prefer to ride, therefore I take care to have near me nothing that can tempt me to overhaul. When anything happens to my machine I wheel it to the nearest repairing shop. If I am too far from the town or village to walk, I sit by the roadside and wait till a cart comes along. My chief danger, I always find, is from the wandering overhauler. The sight of a broken-down machine is

to the overhauler as a wayside corpse to a crow; he swoops down
upon it with a friendly yell of triumph. At first I used to try
politeness. I would say:

'It is nothing; don't you trouble. You ride on, and enjoy
yourself, I beg it of you as a favour; please go away.'

Experience has taught me, however, that courtesy is of no use
in such an extremity. Now I say:

'You go away and leave the thing alone, or I will knock your
silly head off.'

And if you look determined, and have a good stout cudgel in
your hand, you can generally drive him off.

George came in later in the day. He said:

'Well, do you think everything will be ready?'

I said: 'Everything will be ready by Wednesday, except, perhaps, you and Harris.'

He said: 'Is the tandem all right?'

'The tandem,' I said, 'is well.'

He said: 'You don't think it wants overhauling?'

I replied: 'Age and experience have taught me that there are
few matters concerning which a man does well to be positive.
Consequently, there remain to me now but a limited number of
questions upon which I feel any degree of certainty. Among
such still-unshaken beliefs, however, is the conviction that that
tandem does not want overhauling. I also feel a presentiment
that, provided my life is spared, no human being between now
and Wednesday morning is going to overhaul it.'

George said: 'I should not show temper over the matter, if I
were you. There will come a day, perhaps not far distant, when
that bicycle, with a couple of mountains between it and the
nearest repairing shop, will, in spite of your chronic desire for
rest, *have* to be overhauled. Then you will clamour for people
to tell you where you put the oil-can, and what you have done
with the screw-hammer. Then, while you exert yourself
holding the thing steady against a tree, you will suggest that
somebody else should clean the chain and pump the back wheel.'

I felt there was justice in George's rebuke—also a certain
amount of prophetic wisdom. I said:

'Forgive me if I seemed unresponsive. The truth is, Harris
was round here this morning——'

George said: 'Say no more; I understand. Besides, what
I came to talk to you about was another matter. Look at that.'

He handed me a small book bound in red cloth. It was a

guide to English conversation for the use of German travellers. It commenced 'On a Steamboat,' and terminated 'At the Doctor's'; its longest chapter being devoted to conversation in a railway carriage, among, apparently, a compartment load of quarrelsome and ill-mannered lunatics: 'Can you not get farther away from me, sir?'—'It is impossible, madam; my neighbour, here, is very stout'—'Shall we not endeavour to arrange our legs?'—'Please have the goodness to keep your elbows down'— 'Pray do not inconvenience yourself, madam, if my shoulder is of any accommodation to you,' whether intended to be said sarcastically or not, there was nothing to indicate—'I really must request you to move a little, madam, I can hardly breathe,' the author's idea being, presumably, that by this time the whole party was mixed up together on the floor. The chapter concluded with the phrase: 'Here we are at our destination, God be thanked! (*Gott sei dank!*)' a pious exclamation, which under the circumstances must have taken the form of a chorus.

At the end of the book was an appendix, giving the German traveller hints concerning the preservation of his health and comfort during his sojourn in English towns; chief among such hints being advice to him to always travel with a supply of disinfectant powder, to always lock his bedroom door at night, and to always carefully count his small change.

'It is not a brilliant publication,' I remarked, handing the book back to George; 'it is not a book that personally I would recommend to any German about to visit England; I think it would get him disliked.   But I have read books published in London for the use of English travellers abroad every whit as foolish.   Some educated idiot, misunderstanding seven languages, would appear to go about writing these books for the misinformation and false guidance of modern Europe.'

'You cannot deny,' said George, 'that these books are in large request.   They are bought by the thousand, I know.   In every town in Europe there must be people going about talking this sort of thing.'

'Maybe,' I replied; 'but fortunately, nobody understands them.   I have noticed, myself, men standing on railway platforms and at street corners reading aloud from such books. Nobody knows what language they are speaking; nobody has the slightest knowledge of what they are saying.   This is, perhaps, as well; were they understood they would probably be assaulted.'

George said: 'Maybe you are right; my idea is to see what

would happen if they were understood.   My proposal is to get to London early on Wednesday morning, and spend an hour or two going about and shopping with the aid of this book.   There are one or two little things I want—a hat and a pair of bedroom slippers, among other articles.   Our boat does not leave Tilbury till twelve, and that just gives us time.   I want to try this sort of talk where I can properly judge of its effect.   I want to see how the foreigner feels when he is talked to in this way.'

It struck me as a sporting idea.   In my enthusiasm I offered to accompany him, and wait outside the shop.   I said I thought that Harris would like to be in it, too—or rather outside.

George said that was not quite his scheme.   His proposal was that Harris and I should accompany him into the shop.   With Harris, who looks formidable, to support him, and myself at the door to call the police if necessary, he said he was willing to adventure the thing.

We walked round to Harris's, and put the proposal before him. He examined the book, especially the chapters dealing with the purchase of shoes and hats.   He said:

'If George talks to any bootmaker or any hatter the things that are put down here, it is not support he will want; it is carrying to the hospital that he will need.'

That made George angry.

'You talk,' said George, 'as though I were a foolhardy boy without any sense.   I shall select from the more polite and less irritating speeches; the grosser insults I shall avoid.'

This being clearly understood, Harris gave in his adhesion; and our start was fixed for early Wednesday morning.

CHAPTER IV

GEORGE came down on Tuesday evening, and slept at Harris's
place. We thought this a better arrangement than his own suggestion, which was that we should call for him on our way and
'pick him up.' Picking George up in the morning means picking
him out of bed to begin with, and shaking him awake—in itself
an exhausting effort with which to commence the day; helping
him find his things and finish his packing; and then waiting
for him while he eats his breakfast, a tedious entertainment from the
spectator's point of view, full of wearisome repetition.

I knew that if he slept at Beggarbush he would be up in time;
I have slept there myself, and I know what happens. About the
middle of the night, as you judge, though in reality it may be
somewhat later, you are startled out of your first sleep by what
sounds like a rush of cavalry along the passage, just outside your
door. Your half-awakened intelligence fluctuates between
burglars, the Day of Judgment, and a gas explosion. You sit up
in bed and listen intently. You are not kept waiting long; the
next moment a door is violently slammed, and somebody, or
something, is evidently coming downstairs on a tea-tray.

'I told you so,' says a voice outside, and immediately some
hard substance, a head one would say from the ring of it, re-
bounds against the panel of your door.

By this time you are charging madly round the room for your
clothes. Nothing is where you put it overnight, the articles most
essential have disappeared entirely; and meanwhile the murder,
or revolution, or whatever it is, continues unchecked. You
pause for a moment, with your head under the wardrobe, where
you think you can see your slippers, to listen to a steady, monotonous thumping upon a distant door. The victim, you

presume, has taken refuge there; they mean to have him out and finish him. Will you be in time? The knocking ceases, and a voice, sweetly reassuring in its gentle plaintiveness, asks meekly:

'Pa, may I get up?'

You do not hear the other voice, but the responses are:

'No, it was only the bath—no, she ain't really hurt—only wet, you know. Yes, ma, I'll tell 'em what you say. No, it was a pure accident. Yes; good night, papa.'

Then the same voice, exerting itself so as to be heard in a distant part of the house, remarks:

'You've got to come upstairs again. Pa says it isn't time yet to get up.'

You return to bed, and be listening to somebody being dragged upstairs, evidently against their will. By a thoughtful arrangement the spare rooms at Beggarbush are exactly underneath the nurseries. The same somebody, you conclude, still offering the most creditable opposition, is being put back into bed. You can follow the contest with much exactitude, because every time the body is flung down upon the spring mattress, the bedstead, just above your head, makes a sort of jump; while every time the body succeeds in struggling out again, you are aware by the thud upon the floor. After a time the struggle wanes, or maybe the bed collapses; and you drift back into sleep. But the next moment, or what seems to be the next moment, you again open your eyes under the consciousness of a presence. The door is being held ajar, and four solemn faces, piled one on top of the other, are peering at you, as though you were some natural curiosity kept in this particular room. Seeing you awake, the top face, walking calmly over the other three, comes in and sits on the bed in a friendly attitude.

'Oh!' it says, 'we didn't know you were awake. I've been awake some time.'

'So I gather,' you reply shortly.

'Pa doesn't like us to get up too early,' it continues. 'He says everybody else in the house is liable to be disturbed if we get up. So, of course, we mustn't.'

The tone is that of gentle resignation. It is instinct with the spirit of virtuous pride, arising from the consciousness of self-sacrifice.

'Don't you call this being up?' you suggest.

'Oh no; we're not really up, you know, because we're not

properly dressed.' The fact is self-evident. 'Pa's always very tired in the morning,' the voice continues; 'of course, that's because he works hard all day. Are you ever tired in the morning?'

At this point he turns and notices, for the first time, that the three other children have also entered, and are sitting in a semi-circle on the floor. From their attitude it is clear they have mistaken the whole thing for one of the slower forms of entertainment, some comic lecture or conjuring exhibition, and are waiting patiently for you to get out of bed and do something. It shocks him, the idea of their being in the guest's bedchamber. He peremptorily orders them out. They do not answer him, they do not argue; in dead silence, and with one accord they fall upon him. All you can see from the bed is a confused tangle of waving arms and legs, suggestive of an intoxicated octopus trying to find bottom. Not a word is spoken; that seems to be the etiquette of the thing. If you are sleeping in your pyjamas, you spring from the bed, and only add to the confusion; if you are wearing a less showy garment, you stop where you are and shout commands, which are utterly unheeded. The simplest plan is to leave it to the eldest boy. He does get them out after a while, and closes the door upon them. It reopens immediately, and one, generally Muriel, is shot back into the room. She enters as from a catapult. She is handicapped by having long hair, which can be used as a convenient handle. Evidently aware of this natural disadvantage, she clutches it herself tightly in one hand, and punches with the other. He opens the door again, and cleverly uses her as a battering-ram against the wall of those without. You can hear the dull crash as her head enters among them, and scatters them. When the victory is complete, he comes back and resumes his seat on the bed. There is no bitterness about him; he has forgotten the whole incident.

'I like the morning,' he says, 'don't you?'

'Some mornings,' you agree, 'are all right; others are not so peaceful.'

He takes no notice of your exception; a far-away look steals over his somewhat ethereal face.

'I should like to die in the morning,' he says; 'everything is so beautiful then.'

'Well,' you answer, 'perhaps you will, if your father ever invites an irritable man to come and sleep here, and doesn't warn him beforehand.'

He descends from his contemplative mood, and becomes himself again.

'It's jolly in the garden,' he suggests; 'you wouldn't like to get up and have a game of cricket, would you?'

It was not the idea with which you went to bed, but now, as things have turned out, it seems as good a plan as lying there hopelessly awake; and you agree.

You learn, later in the day, that the explanation of the proceeding is that you, unable to sleep, woke up early in the morning, and thought you would like a game of cricket. The children, taught to be ever courteous to guests, felt it their duty to humour you. Mrs Harris remarks at breakfast that at least you might have seen to it that the children were properly dressed before you took them out; while Harris points out to you, pathetically, how by your one morning's example and encouragement, you have undone his labour of months.

On this Wednesday morning, George, it seems, clamoured to get up at a quarter past five, and persuaded them to let him teach them cycling tricks round the cucumber frames on Harris's new wheel. Even Mrs Harris, however, did not blame George on this occasion; she felt intuitively the idea would not have been entirely his.

It is not that the Harris children have the faintest notion of avoiding blame at the expense of a friend and comrade. One and all they are honesty itself in accepting responsibility for their own misdeeds. It simply is, that is how the thing presents itself to their understanding. When you explain to them that you had no original intention of getting up at five o'clock in the morning to play cricket on the croquet lawn, or to mimic the history of the early Church by shooting with a crossbow at dolls tied to a tree; that as a matter of fact, left to your own initiative, you would have slept peacefully till roused in Christian fashion with a cup of tea at eight, they are firstly astonished, secondly apologetic, and thirdly sincerely contrite. In the present instance, waiving the purely academic question whether the awakening of George at a little before five was due to natural instinct on his part, or to the accidental passing of a home-made boomerang through his bedroom window, the dear children frankly admitted that the blame for his uprising was their own. As the eldest boy said:

'We ought to have remembered that Uncle George had a long day before him, and we ought to have dissuaded him from getting up. I blame myself entirely.'

But an occasional change of habit does nobody any harm; and besides, as Harris and I agreed, it was good training for George. In the Black Forest we should be up at five every morning; that we had determined on.   Indeed, George himself had suggested half past four, but Harris and I had argued that five would be early enough as an average; that would enable us to be on our machines by six, and to break the back of our journey before the heat of the day set in.   Occasionally, we might start a little earlier, but not as a habit.

I myself was up that morning at five.   This was earlier than I had intended.   I had said to myself on going to sleep, 'Six o'clock, sharp!'

There are men I know who can wake themselves at any time to the minute.   They say to themselves literally, as they lay their heads upon the pillow, 'Four-thirty,' 'Four-forty-five,' or 'Five-fifteen,' as the case may be; and as the clock strikes they open their eyes.   It is very wonderful this; the more one dwells upon it, the greater the mystery grows.   Some Ego within us, acting quite independently of our conscious self, must be capable of counting the hours while we sleep.   Unaided by clock or sun, or any other medium known to our five senses, it keeps watch through the darkness.   At the exact moment it whispers 'Time!' and we awake.   The work of an old riverside fellow I once talked with called him to be out of bed each morning half an hour before high tide.   He told me that never once had he overslept himself by a minute.   Latterly, he never even troubled to work out the tide for himself.   He would lie down tired, and sleep a dreamless sleep, and each morning at a different hour this ghostly watch-man, true as the tide itself, would silently call him.   Did the man's spirit haunt through the darkness the muddy river stairs; or had it knowledge of the ways of Nature?   Whatever the process, the man himself was unconscious of it.

In my own case my inward watchman is, perhaps, somewhat out of practice.   He does his best; but he is over-anxious; he worries himself, and loses count.   I say to him, maybe, 'Five-thirty, please'; and he wakes me with a start at half past two. I look at my watch.   He suggests that, perhaps, I forgot to wind it up.   I put it to my ear; it is still going.   He thinks, maybe, something has happened to it; he is confident himself it is half past five, if not a little later.   To satisfy him, I put on a pair of slippers and go downstairs to inspect the dining-room clock. What happens to a man when he wanders about the house in the middle of the night, clad in a dressing-gown and a pair of slippers, there is no need to recount; most men know by experience. Everything—especially everything with a sharp corner—takes a cowardly delight in hitting him. When you are wearing a pair of stout boots, things get out of your way; when you venture among furniture in woolwork slippers and no socks, it comes at you and kicks you. I return to bed bad tempered, and refusing to listen to his further absurd suggestion that all the clocks in the house have entered into a conspiracy against me, take half an hour to get to sleep again. From four to five he wakes me every ten minutes. I wish I had never said a word to him about the thing. At five o'clock he goes to sleep himself, worn out, and leaves it to the girl, who does it half an hour later than usual.

On this particular Wednesday he worried me to such an extent, that I got up at five simply to be rid of him. I did not know what to do with myself. Our train did not leave till eight; all our luggage had been packed and sent on the night before, together with the bicycles, to Fenchurch Street station. I went into my study; I thought I would put in an hour's writing. The early morning, before one has breakfasted, is not, I take it, a good season for literary effort. I wrote three paragraphs of a story, and then read them over to myself. Some unkind things have been said about my work; but nothing has yet been written which would have done justice to those three paragraphs. I threw them into the waste-paper basket, and sat trying to remember what, if any, charitable institutions provided pensions for decayed authors.

To escape from this train of reflection, I put a golf-ball in my pocket, and selecting a driver, strolled out into the paddock. A couple of sheep were browsing there, and they followed and took a keen interest in my practice. The one was a kindly, sympathetic old party. I do not think she understood the game; I think it was my doing this innocent thing so early in the morning that appealed to her. At every stroke I made she bleated:

'Go—o—o—d, go—o—o—d ind—e—e—d!'

She seemed as pleased as if she had done it herself.

As for the other one, she was a cantankerous, disagreeable old thing, as discouraging to me as her friend was helpful.

'Ba—a—a—d, da—a—a—m ba—a—a—d!' was her comment on almost every stroke. As a matter of fact, some were really excellent strokes; but she did it just to be contradictory, and for the sake of irritating. I could see that.

By a most regrettable accident, one of my swiftest balls struck the good sheep on the nose. And at that the bad sheep laughed —laughed distinctly and undoubtedly, a husky, vulgar laugh; and, while her friend stood glued to the ground, too astonished to move, she changed her note for the first time and bleated:

'Go—o—o—d, ve—e—ry go—o—o—d! Be—e—e—est sho—o—o—ot he—e—e's ma—a—a—de!'

I would have given half a crown if it had been she I had hit instead of the other one. It is ever the good and amiable who suffer in this world.

I had wasted more time than I had intended in the paddock, and when Ethelbertha came to tell me it was half past seven, and the breakfast was on the table, I remembered that I had not shaved. It vexes Ethelbertha my shaving quickly. She fears that to outsiders it may suggest a poor-spirited attempt at suicide, and that in consequence it may get about the neighbourhood that we are not happy together. As a further argument, she has also hinted that my appearance is not of the kind that can be trifled with.

On the whole, I was just as glad not to be able to take a long farewell of Ethelbertha; I did not want to risk her breaking down. But I should have liked more opportunity to say a few farewell words of advice to the children, especially as regards my fishing-rod, which they will persist in using for cricket stumps; and I hate having to run for a train. Quarter of a mile from the station I overtook George and Harris; they were also running. In their case—so Harris informed me, jerkily, while we trotted side by side—it was the new kitchen stove that was to blame. This was the first morning they had tried it, and from some cause or other it had blown up the kidneys and scalded the cook. He said he hoped that by the time we returned they would have got more used to it.

We caught the train by the skin of our teeth, as the saying is, and reflecting upon the events of the morning, as we sat gasping in the carriage, there passed vividly before my mind the panorama of my Uncle Podger, as on two hundred and fifty days in the year he would start from Ealing Common by the nine-thirteen train to Moorgate Street.

From my Uncle Podger's house to the railway station was eight minutes' walk. What my uncle always said was:

'Allow yourself a quarter of an hour, and take it easily.'

What he always did was to start five minutes before the time

My Uncle Podger runs for his train

and run. I do not know why, but this was the custom of the suburb. Many stout City gentlemen lived at Ealing in those days—I believe some live there still—and caught early trains to Town. They all started late; they all carried a black bag and a newspaper in one hand, and an umbrella in the other; and for the last quarter of a mile to the station, wet or fine, they all ran.

Folks with nothing else to do, nursemaids chiefly and errand boys, with now and then a perambulating costermonger added, would gather on the common of a fine morning to watch them pass, and cheer the most deserving. It was not a showy spectacle. They did not run well, they did not even run fast; but they were earnest, and they did their best. The exhibition appealed less to one's sense of art than to one's natural admiration for conscientious effort.

Occasionally a little harmless betting would take place among the crowd.

'Two to one agin the old gent in the white weskit!'

'Ten to one on old Blowpipes, bar he don't roll over hisself 'fore 'e gets there!'

'Heven money on the Purple Hemperor!'—a nickname bestowed by a youth of entomological tastes upon a certain retired military neighbour of my uncle's—a gentleman of imposing appearance when stationary, but apt to colour highly under exercise.

My uncle and the others would write to the *Ealing Press* complaining bitterly concerning the supineness of the local police; and the editor would add spirited leaders upon the Decay of Courtesy among the Lower Orders, especially throughout the western suburbs. But no good ever resulted.

It was not that my uncle did not rise early enough; it was that troubles came to him at the last moment. The first thing he would do after breakfast would be to lose his newspaper. We always knew when Uncle Podger had lost anything, by the expression of astonished indignation with which, on such occasions, he would regard the world in general. It never occurred to my Uncle Podger to say to himself:

'I am a careless old man. I lose everything: I never know where I have put anything. I am quite incapable of finding it again for myself. In this respect I must be a perfect nuisance to everybody about me. I must set to work and reform myself.'

On the contrary, by some peculiar course of reasoning, he had convinced himself that whenever he lost a thing it was everybody else's fault in the house but his own.

'I had it in my hand here not a minute ago!' he would exclaim.

From his tone you would have thought he was living surrounded by conjurers, who spirited away things from him merely to irritate him.

'Could you have left it in the garden?' my aunt would suggest.

'What should I want to leave it in the garden for? I don't want a paper in the garden; I want the paper in the train with me.'

'You haven't put it in your pocket?'

'God bless the woman! Do you think I should be standing here at five minutes to nine looking for it if I had it in my pocket all the while? *Do* you think I'm a fool?'

Here somebody would explain, 'What's this?' and hand him from somewhere a paper neatly folded.

'I do wish people would leave my things alone,' he would growl, snatching at it savagely.

He would open his bag to put it in, and then glancing at it, he would pause, speechless with sense of injury.

'What's the matter?' aunt would ask.

'The day before yesterday's!' he would answer, too hurt even to shout, throwing the paper down upon the table.

If only sometimes it had been yesterday's it would have been a change. But it was always the day before yesterday's; except on Tuesday; then it would be Saturday's.

We would find it for him eventually; as often as not he was sitting on it. And then he would smile, not genially, but with the weariness that comes to a man who feels that fate has cast his lot among a band of hopeless idiots.

'All the time, right in front of your noses——!' He would not finish the sentence; he prided himself on his self-control.

This settled, he would start for the hall, where it was the custom of my Aunt Maria to have the children gathered, ready to say good-bye to him.

My aunt never left the house herself, if only to make a call next door, without taking a tender farewell of every inmate. One never knew, she would say, what might happen.

One of them, of course, was sure to be missing, and the moment this was noticed all the other six, without an instant's hesitation, would scatter with a whoop to find it. Immediately they were gone it would turn up by itself from somewhere quite near, always with the most reasonable explanation for its absence; and would at once start off after the others to explain to them that it was found.   In this way, five minutes at least would be taken up in everybody's looking for everybody else, which was just sufficient time to allow my uncle to find his umbrella and lose his hat.   Then, at last, the group reassembled in the hall, the drawing-room clock would commence to strike nine.   It possessed a cold, penetrating chime that always had the effect of confusing my uncle.   In his excitement he would kiss some of the children twice over, pass by others, forget whom he had kissed and whom he hadn't, and have to begin all over again. He used to say he believed they mixed themselves up on purpose, and I am not prepared to maintain that the charge was altogether false.   To add to his troubles, one child always had a sticky face and that child would always be the most affectionate.

If things were going too smoothly, the eldest boy would come out with some tale about all the clocks in the house being five minutes slow, and of his having been late for school the previous day in consequence.   This would send my uncle rushing impetuously down to the gate, where he would recollect that he had with him neither his bag nor his umbrella.   All the children that my aunt could not stop would charge after him, two of them struggling for the umbrella, the others surging round the bag. And when they returned we would discover on the hall table the most important thing of all that he had forgotten, and wondered what he would say about it when he came home.

We arrived at Waterloo a little after nine, and at once proceeded to put George's experiment into operation.   Opening the book at the chapter entitled 'At the Cab Rank,' we walked up to a hansom, raised our hats, and wished the driver 'Good morning.'

This man was not to be outdone in politeness by any foreigner, real or imitation.   Calling to a friend named 'Charles' to 'hold the steed,' he sprang from his box, and returned to us a bow that would have done credit to Mr Turveydrop himself.   Speaking apparently in the name of the nation, he welcomed us to England, adding a regret that Her Majesty was not at the moment in London.

We could not reply to him in kind.   Nothing of this sort had been anticipated by the book.   We called him 'coachman,' at which he again bowed to the pavement, and asked him if he would have the goodness to drive us to the Westminster Bridge Road.

He laid his hand upon his heart, and said the pleasure would be his.

Taking the third sentence in the chapter, George asked him what his fare would be.

The question, as introducing a sordid element into the conversation, seemed to hurt his feelings. He said he never took money from distinguished strangers; he suggested a souvenir—a diamond scarf pin, a gold snuffbox, some little trifle of that sort by which he could remember us.

As a small crowd had collected, and as the joke was drifting rather too far in the cabman's direction, we climbed in without further parley, and were driven away amid cheers. We stopped the cab at a boot shop a little past Astley's Theatre that looked the sort of place we wanted. It was one of those overfed shops that the moment their shutters are taken down in the morning disgorge their goods all round them. Boxes of boots stood piled on the pavement or in the gutter opposite. Boots hung in festoons about its doors and windows. Its sunblind was as some grimy vine, bearing bunches of black and brown boots. Inside, the shop was a bower of boots. The man, when we entered, was busy with a chisel and hammer opening a new crate full of boots.

George raised his hat, and said 'Good morning.'

The man did not even turn round. He struck me from the first as a disagreeable man. He grunted something which might have been 'Good morning,' or might not, and went on with his work.

George said: 'I have been recommended to your shop by my friend, Mr X.'

In response, the man should have said: 'Mr X is a most worthy gentleman; it will give me the greatest pleasure to serve any friend of his.'

What he did say was: 'Don't know him; never heard of him.'

This was disconcerting. The book gave three or four methods of buying boots; George had carefully selected the one centred round 'Mr X,' as being of all the most courtly. You talked a good deal with the shopkeeper about this 'Mr X,' and then, when by this means friendship and understanding had been established, you slid naturally and gracefully into the immediate object of your coming, namely, your desire for boots, 'cheap and good.' This gross, material man cared, apparently, nothing for the niceties of retail dealing. It was necessary with such a one to come to business with brutal directness. George abandoned 'Mr X,' and turning back to a previous page, took a sentence at random. It was not a happy selection; it was a speech that would have been superfluous made to any bootmaker. Under the present circumstances, threatened and stifled as we were on every side by boots, it possessed the dignity of positive imbecility. It ran: 'One has told me that you have here boots for sale.'

For the first time the man put down his hammer and chisel, and looked at us. He spoke slowly, in a thick and husky voice. He said:

'What d'ye think I keep boots for—to smell 'em?'

He was one of those men that begin quietly and grow more angry as they proceed, their wrongs apparently working within them like yeast.

'What d'ye think I am,' he continued, 'a boot collector? What d'ye think I'm running this shop for—my health? D'ye think I love the boots, and can't bear to part with a pair? D'ye think I hang 'em about here to look at 'em? Ain't there enough of 'em? Where d'ye think you are—in an international exhi- bition of boots? What d'ye think these boots are—a historical collection? Did you ever hear of a man keeping a boot shop and not selling boots? D'ye think I decorate the shop with 'em to make it look pretty? What d'ye take me for—a prize idiot?'

I have always maintained that these conversation books are never of any real use. What we wanted was some English equivalent for the well-known German idiom: 'Behalten Sie Ihr Haar auf.'

Nothing of the sort was to be found in the book from begin- ning to end. However, I will do George the credit to admit he chose the very best sentence that was to be found therein and applied it. He said:

'I will come again, when, perhaps, you will have some more boots to show me. Till then, adieu!'

With that we returned to our cab and drove away, leaving the man standing in the centre of his boot-bedecked doorway addres- sing remarks to us. What he said, I did not hear, but the passers- by appeared to find it interesting.

George was for stopping at another boot shop and trying the experiment afresh; he said he really did want a pair of bedroom slippers. But we persuaded him to postpone their purchase until our arrival in some foreign city, where the tradespeople are no doubt more inured to this sort of talk, or else more naturally amiable. On the subject of the hat, however, he was adamant.

He maintained that without that he could not travel, and, accordingly, we pulled up at a small shop in the Blackfriars Road.

The proprietor of this shop was a cheery, bright-eyed little man, and he helped us rather than hindered us.

When George asked him in the words of the book: 'Have you any hats?' he did not get angry; he just stopped and thoughtfully scratched his chin.

'Hats,' said he. 'Let me think. Yes'—here a smile of positive pleasure broke over his genial countenance—'yes, now I come to think of it, I believe I have a hat. But, tell me, why do you ask me?'

George explained to him that he wished to purchase a cap, a travelling cap, but the essence of the transaction was that it was to be a 'good cap.'

The man's face fell.

'Ah,' he remarked, 'there, I am afraid, you have me. Now, if you had wanted a bad cap, not worth the price asked for it; a cap good for nothing but to clean windows with, I could have found you the very thing. But a good cap—no; we don't keep them. But wait a minute,' he continued, on seeing the disappointment that spread over George's expressive countenance, 'don't be in a hurry. I have a cap here'—he went to a drawer and opened it—'it is not a good cap, but it is not so bad as most of the caps I sell.'

He brought it forward, extended on his palm.

'What do you think of that?' he asked. 'Could you put up with that?'

George fitted it on before the glass, and, choosing another remark from the book, said:

'This hat fits me sufficiently well, but, tell me, do you consider that it becomes me?'

The man stepped back and took a bird's-eye view.

'Candidly,' he replied, 'I can't say that it does.'

He turned from George, and addressed himself to Harris and myself.

'Your friend's beauty,' said he, 'I should describe as elusive. It is there, but you can easily miss it. Now, in that cap, to my mind, you do miss it.'

At that point it occurred to George that he had had sufficient fun with this particular man. He said:

'That is all right. We don't want to lose the train. How much?'

Answered the man: 'The price of that cap, sir, which, in my opinion, is twice as much as it is worth, is four-and-six. Would you like it wrapped up in brown paper, sir, or in white?'

George said he would take it as it was, paid the man four-and-six in silver, and went out. Harris and I followed.

At Fenchurch Street we compromised with our cabman for five shillings. He made us another courtly bow, and begged us to remember him to the Emperor of Austria.

Comparing views in the train, we agreed that we had lost the game by two points to one; and George, who was evidently disappointed, threw the book out of the window.

We found our luggage and the bicycles safe on the boat, and with the tide at twelve dropped down the river.

CHAPTER V

A STORY is told of a Scotchman who, loving a lassie, desired her for his wife. But he possessed the prudence of his race. He had noticed in his circle many an otherwise promising union result in disappointment and dismay, purely in consequence of the false estimate formed by bride or bridegroom concerning the imagined perfectability of the other. He determined that in his own case no collapsed ideal should be possible. Therefore, it was that his proposal took the following form:

'I'm but a puir lad, Jennie; I hae nae siller to offer ye, and nae land.'

'Ah, but ye hae yoursel', Davie!'

'An I'm wishfu' it wa' onything else, lassie. I'm nae but a puir ill-seasoned loon, Jennie.'

'Na, na; there's mony a lad mair ill-looking than yoursel', Davie.'

'I hae na seen him, lass, and I'm just a-thinkin' I should na' care to.'

'Better a plain man, Davie, that ye can depend a' than ane that would be a speirin' at the lassies, a-bringin' trouble into the hame wi' his flouting ways.'

'Dinna ye reckon on that, Jennie; it's nae the bonniest Bubbly Jock that mak's the most feathers to fly in the kailyard. I was ever a lad to run after the petticoats, as is weel kent; an' it's a weary handfu' I'll be to ye, I'm thinkin'.'

'Ah, but ye hae a kind heart, Davie! an' ye love me weel. I'm sure on't.'

'I like ye weel enoo', Jennie, though I canna say how long the feeling may bide wi' me; an' I'm kind enoo' when I hae my ain way, an' naethin' happens to put me oot. But I hae the deevil's ain temper, as my mither can tell ye, an' like my puir fayther, I'm a-thinkin', I'll grow nae better as I grow mair auld.'

'Ay, but ye're sair hard upon yersel', Davie.   Ye're an honest lad.   I ken ye better than ye ken yersel', an' ye'll mak a guid hame for me.'

'Maybe, Jennie!   But I hae my doots.   It's a sair thing for

Davie proposes

wife an' bairns when the guid man canna keep awa' frae the glass; an' when the scent of the whusky comes to me it's just as though I hae'd the throat o' a Loch Tay salmon; it just gaes doon an' doon, an' there's nae filling o' me.'

'Ay, but ye're a guid man when ye're sober.   Davie.'

'Maybe I'll be that, Jennie, if I'm nae disturbed.'

'An' ye'll bide wi' me, Davie, an' work for me?'

'I see nae reason why I shouldna bide wi' ye, Jennie; but dinna ye clack aboot work to me, for I just canna bear the thocht o't.'

'Anyhow, ye'll do your best, Davie? As the minister says, nae man can do mair than that.'

'An' it's a puir best that mine'll be, Jennie, and I'm nae sae sure ye'll hae ower muckle even o' that. We're a' weak, sinfu' creatures, Jennie, an' ye'd hae some deefficulty to find a man weaker or mair sinfu' than mysel'.'

'Weel, weel, ye hae a truthfu' tongue, Davie. Mony a lad will mak fine promises to a puir lassie, only to break 'em an' her heart wi' 'em. Ye speak me fair, Davie, and I'm thinkin' I'll just tak ye, an' see what comes o't.'

Concerning what did come of it, the story is silent, but one feels that under no circumstances had the lady any right to complain of her bargain. Whether she ever did or did not—for women do not invariably order their tongues according to logic, nor men either for the matter of that—Davie, himself, must have had the satisfaction of reflecting that all reproaches were undeserved.

I wish to be equally frank with the reader of this book. I wish here conscientiously to let forth its shortcomings. I wish no one to read this book under a misapprehension.

There will be no useful information in this book.

Anyone who should think that with the aid of this book he would be able to make a tour through Germany and the Black Forest would probably lose himself before he got to the Nore. That, at all events, would be the best thing that could happen to him. The farther away from home he got, the greater only would be his difficulties.

I do not regard the conveyance of useful information as my *forte*. This belief was not inborn with me; it has been driven home upon me by experience.

In my early journalistic days, I served upon a paper, the forerunner of many very popular periodicals of the present day. Our boast was that we combined instruction with amusement; as to what should be regarded as affording amusement and what instruction, the reader judged for himself. We gave advice to people about to marry—long, earnest advice that would, had they followed it, have made our circle of readers the envy of the whole married world. We told our subscribers how to make fortunes by keeping rabbits, giving facts and figures. The thing that must have surprised them was that we ourselves did not give up journalism and start rabbit-farming. Often and often have I proved conclusively from authoritative sources how a man starting a rabbit farm with twelve selected rabbits and a little judgment must, at the end of three years, be in receipt of an income of two thousand a year, rising rapidly; he simply could not help himself. He might not want the money. He might not know what to do with it when he had it. But there it was for him. I have never met a rabbit farmer myself worth two thousand a year, though I have known many start with the twelve necessary, assorted rabbits. Something has always gone wrong somewhere; maybe the continued atmosphere of a rabbit farm saps the judgment.

We told our readers how many bald-headed men there were in Iceland, and for all we knew our figures may have been correct; how many red herrings placed tail to mouth it would take to reach from London to Rome, which must have been useful to anyone desirous of laying down a line of red herrings from London to Rome, enabling him to order in the right quantity at the beginning; how many words the average woman spoke in a day; and other suchlike items of information calculated to make them wise and great beyond the readers of other journals.

We told them how to cure fits in cats. Personally I do not believe, and I did not believe then, that you can cure fits in cats. If I had a cat subject to fits I should advertise it for sale, or even give it away. But our duty was to supply information when asked for. Some fool wrote, clamouring to know; and I spent the best part of a morning seeking knowledge on the subject. I found what I wanted at length at the end of an old cookery book. What it was doing there I have never been able to understand. It had nothing to do with the proper subject of the book whatever; there was no suggestion that you could make anything savoury out of a cat, even when you had cured it of its fits. The authoress had just thrown in this paragraph out of pure generosity. I can only say that I wish she had left it out; it was the cause of a deal of angry correspondence and of the loss of four subscribers to the paper, if not more. The man said the result of following our advice had been two pounds worth of damage to his kitchen crockery, to say nothing of a broken window and probable blood poisoning to himself; added to which the cat's fits were worse than before. And yet it was a simple enough recipe. You held the cat between your legs, gently, so as not to hurt it, and with a pair of scissors made a sharp, clean cut in its tail. You did not cut off any part of the tail; you were to be careful not to do that; you only made an incision.

As we explained to the man, the garden or the coal cellar would have been the proper place for the operation; no one but an idiot would have attempted to perform it in a kitchen, and without help.

We gave them hints on etiquette. We told them how to address peers and bishops; how to eat soup. We instructed shy young men how to acquire easy grace in drawing-rooms. We taught dancing to both sexes by the aid of diagrams. We solved their religious doubts for them, and supplied them with a code of morals that would have done credit to a stained-glass window.

The paper was not a financial success, it was some years before its time, and the consequence was that our staff was limited. My own department, I remember, included 'Advice to Mothers' —I wrote that with the assistance of my landlady, who, having divorced one husband and buried four children, was, I considered, a reliable authority on all domestic matters: 'Hints on Furnishing and Household Decorations—with Designs'; a column of 'Literary Counsel to Beginners'—I sincerely hope my guidance was of better service to them than it has ever proved to myself; and our weekly article, 'Straight Talks to Young Men,' signed 'Uncle Henry.' A kindly, genial old fellow was 'Uncle Henry,' with wide and varied experience, and a sympathetic attitude towards the rising generation. He had been through trouble himself in his far back youth, and knew most things. Even to this day I read 'Uncle Henry's' advice, and, though I say it who should not, it still seems to me good, sound advice. I often think that had I followed 'Uncle Henry's' counsel closer I would have been wiser, made fewer mistakes, felt better satisfied with myself than is now the case.

A quiet, weary little woman, who lived in a bed-sitting room off the Tottenham Court Road, and who had a husband in a lunatic asylum, did our 'Cooking Column,' 'Hints on Education' —we were full of Hints—and a page and a half of 'Fashionable Intelligence,' written in the pertly personal style which even yet has not altogether disappeared, so I am informed, from modern journalism: 'I must tell you about the *divine* frock I wore at "Glorious Goodwood" last week. Prince C.—but there, I really must *not* repeat all the things the silly fellow says; he is *too* foolish—and the *dear* Countess, I fancy, was just the *weeish* bit jealous'—and so on.

Poor little woman! I see her now in the shabby grey alpaca, with the inkstains on it. Perhaps a day at 'Glorious Goodwood,' or anywhere else in the fresh air, might have put some colour into her cheeks.

Our proprietor—one of the most unashamedly ignorant men I ever met—I remember his gravely informing a correspondent once that Ben Jonson had written *Rabelais* to pay for his mother's funeral, and only laughing good-naturedly when his mistakes were pointed out to him—wrote with the aid of a cheap encyclopaedia the pages devoted to 'General Information,' and did them on the whole remarkably well; while our office boy, with an excellent pair of scissors for his assistant, was responsible for our supply of 'Wit and Humour.'

It was hard work, and the pay was poor, what sustained us was the consciousness that we were instructing and improving our fellow men and women. Of all games in the world, the one most universally and eternally popular is the game of school. You collect six children, and put them on a doorstep, while you walk up and down with the book and cane. We play it when babies, we play it when boys and girls, we play it when men and women, we play it as, lean and slippered, we totter towards the grave. It never palls upon, it never wearies us. Only one thing mars it: the tendency of one and all of the other six children to clamour for their turn with the book and the cane. The reason, I am sure, that journalism is so popular a calling, in spite of its many drawbacks, is this: each journalist feels he is the boy walking up and down with the cane. The Government, the Classes, and the Masses, Society, Art, and Literature, are the other children sitting on the doorstep. He instructs and improves them.

But I digress. It was to excuse my present permanent disinclination to be the vehicle of useful information that I recalled these matters. Let us now return.

Somebody, signing himself 'Balloonist,' had written to ask concerning the manufacture of hydrogen gas. It is an easy thing to manufacture—at least, so I gathered after reading up the subject at the British Museum; yet I did warn 'Balloonist,' whoever he might be, to take all necessary precaution against accident. What more could I have done? Ten days afterwards a florid-faced lady called at the office, leading by the hand what, she explained, was her son, aged twelve. The boy's face was unimpressive to a degree positively remarkable. His mother pushed him forward and took off his hat, and then I perceived the reason for this. He had no eyebrows whatever, and of his hair nothing remained but a scrubby dust, giving to his head the appearance of a hard-boiled egg, skinned and sprinkled with black pepper.

'That was a handsome lad this time last week, with naturally

'*That was a handsome lad this time last week*'

curly hair,' remarked the lady.   She spoke with a rising inflection, suggestive of the beginning of things.

'What has happened to him?' asked our chief.

'This is what's happened to him,' retorted the lady.   She drew from her muff a copy of our last week's issue, with my article on hydrogen gas scored in pencil, and flung it before his eyes.   Our chief took it and read it through.

'He was "Balloonist"?' queried the chief.

'He was "Balloonist,"' admitted the lady, 'the poor innocent child, and now look at him!'

'Maybe it'll grow again,' suggested our chief.

'Maybe it will,' retorted the lady, her key continuing to rise, 'and maybe it won't. What I want to know is what you are going to do for him.'

Our chief suggested a hair wash. I thought at first she was going to fly at him; but for the moment she confined herself to words. It appears she was not thinking of a hair wash, but of compensation. She also made observations on the general character of our paper, its utility, its claim to public support, the sense and wisdom of its contributors.

'I really don't see that it is our fault,' urged the chief—he was a mild-mannered man; 'he asked for information, and he got it.'

'Don't you try to be funny about it,' said the lady (he had not meant to be funny, I am sure; levity was not his failing) 'or you'll get something that *you* haven't asked for. Why, for two pins,' said the lady, with a suddenness that sent us both flying like scuttled chickens behind our respective chairs, 'I'd come round and make your head like it!' I take it, she meant like the boy's. She also added observations upon our chief's personal appearance that were distinctly in bad taste. She was not a nice woman by any means.

Myself, I am of opinion that had she brought the action she threatened, she would have had no case; but our chief was a man who had had experience of the law, and his principle was always to avoid it. I have heard him say:

'If a man stopped me in the street and demanded of me my watch, I should refuse to give it to him. If he threatened to take it by force, I feel I should, though not a fighting man, do my best to protect it. If, on the other hand, he should assert his intention of trying to obtain it by means of an action in any court of law, I should take it out of my pocket and hand it to him, and think I had got off cheaply.'

He squared the matter with the florid-faced lady for a five-pound note, which must have represented a month's profits on the paper; and she departed, taking her damaged offspring with her. After she was gone, our chief spoke kindly to me. He said:

'Don't think I am blaming you in the least; it is not your fault, it is Fate. Keep to moral advice and criticism—there you are distinctly good; but don't try your hand any more on "Useful Information." As I have said, it is not your fault. Your information is correct enough—there is nothing to be said against that; it simply is that you are not lucky with it.'

I would that I had followed his advice always; I would have saved myself and other people much disaster. I see no reason why it should be, but so it is. If I instruct a man as to the best route between London and Rome, he loses his luggage in Switzerland, or is nearly shipwrecked off Dover. If I counsel him in the purchase of a camera, he gets run in by the German police for photographing fortresses. I once took a deal of trouble to explain to a man how to marry his deceased wife's sister at Stockholm. I found out for him the time the boat left Hull and the best hotels to stop at. There was not a single mistake from beginning to end in the information with which I supplied him; no hitch occurred anywhere; yet now he never speaks to me.

Therefore it is that I have come to restrain my passion for the giving of information; therefore it is that nothing in the nature of practical instruction will be found, if I can help it, within these pages.

There will be no description of towns, no historical reminiscenses, no architecture, no morals.

I once asked an intelligent foreigner what he thought of London.

He said: 'It is a very big town.'

I said: 'What struck you most about it?'

He replied: 'The people.'

I said: 'Compared with other towns—Paris, Rome, Berlin—what did you think of it?'

He shrugged his shoulders. 'It is bigger,' he said; 'what more can one say?'

One ant-hill is very much like another. So many avenues, wide or narrow, where the little creatures swarm in strange confusion; these bustling by, important; these halting to pow-wow with one another. These struggling with big burdens; those but basking in the sun. So many granaries stored with food; so many cells where the little things sleep, and eat, and love; the corner where lie their little white bones. This hive is larger, the next smaller. This nest lies on the sand, and another under the stones. This was built but yesterday, while that was fashioned ages ago, some say even before the swallows came; who knows?

Nor will there be found herein folk-lore or story.

Every valley where lie homesteads has its song. I will tell you the plot; you can turn it into verse and set it to music of your own.

There lived a lass, and there came a lad, who loved and rode away.

It is a monotonous song, written in many languages; for the young man seems to have been a mighty traveller. Here in sentimental Germany they remember him well. So also the dwellers of the Blue Alsatian Mountains remember his coming among them; while, if my memory serves me truly, he likewise visited the Banks of Allan Water. A veritable Wandering Jew is he; for still the foolish girls listen, so they say, to the dying away of his hoof-beats.

In this land of many ruins, that long while ago were voice-filled homes, linger many legends; and here again, giving you the essentials, I leave you to cook the dish for yourself. Take a human heart or two, assorted; a bundle of human passions—there are not many of them, half a dozen at the most; season with a mixture of good and evil; flavour the whole with the sauce of death, and serve up where and when you will. 'The Saint's Cell,' 'The Haunted Keep,' 'The Dungeon Grave,' 'The Lover's Leap'—call it what you will, the stew's the same.

Lastly, in this book there will be no scenery. This is not laziness on my part; it is self-control. Nothing is easier to write than scenery; nothing more difficult and unnecessary to read. When Gibbon had to trust to travellers' tales for a description of the Hellespont, and the Rhine was chiefly familiar to English students through the medium of Caesar's *Commentaries*, it behoved every globe-trotter, for whatever distance, to describe to the best of his ability the things that he had seen. Dr John-son, familiar with little else than the view down Fleet Street, could read the description of a Yorkshire moor with pleasure and with profit. To a cockney who had never seen higher ground than the Hog's Back in Surrey, an account of Snowdon must have appeared exciting. But we, or rather the steam-engine and the camera for us, have changed all that. The man who plays tennis every year at the foot of the Matterhorn, and billiards on the summit of the Rigi, does not thank you for an elaborate and painstaking description of the Grampian Hills. To the average man, who has seen a dozen oil-paintings, a hundred photographs, a thousand pictures in the illustrated journals, and a couple of panoramas of Niagara, the word-painting of a waterfall is tedious.

An American friend of mine, a cultured gentleman, who loved poetry well enough for its own sake, told me that he had obtained a more correct and more satisfying idea of the Lake district from an eighteenpenny book of photographic views than from all the words of Coleridge, Southey, and Wordsworth put together. I also remember his saying concerning this subject of scenery in literature, that he would thank an author as much for writing an eloquent description of what he had just had for dinner. But this was in reference to another argument; namely, the proper province of each art. My friend maintained that just as canvas and colour were the wrong mediums for story telling, so word-painting was, at its best, but a clumsy method of conveying impressions that could much better be received through the eye.

As regards the question, there also lingers in my memory very distinctly a hot school afternoon. The class was for English literature, and the proceedings commenced with the reading of a certain lengthy, but otherwise unobjectionable, poem. The author's name, I am ashamed to say, I have forgotten, together with the title of the poem. The reading finished, we closed our books, and the Professor, a kindly, white-haired old gentleman, suggested our giving in our own words an account of what we had just read.

'Tell me,' said the Professor encouragingly, 'what it is all about.'

'Please, sir,' said the first boy—he spoke with bowed head and evident reluctance, as though the subject were one which, left to himself, he would never have mentioned—'it is about a maiden.'

'Yes,' agreed the Professor; 'but I want you to tell me in your own words. We do not speak of a maiden, you know; we say a girl. Yes, it is about a girl. Go on.'

'A girl,' repeated the top boy, the substitution apparently increasing his embarrassment, 'who lived in a wood.'

'What sort of a wood?' asked the Professor.

The first boy examined his ink-pot carefully, and then looked at the ceiling.

'Come,' urged the Professor, growing impatient, 'you have been reading about this wood for the last ten minutes. Surely you can tell me something concerning it.'

'The gnarly trees, their twisted branches'—recommenced the top boy.

'No, no,' interrupted the Professor. 'I do not want you to repeat the poem. I want you to tell me in your own words what sort of a wood it was where the girl lived.'

The Professor tapped his foot impatiently; the top boy made a dash for it.

'Please, sir, it was the usual sort of a wood.'

'Tell him what sort of a wood,' said he, pointing to the second lad.

The second boy said it was a 'green wood.' This annoyed the Professor still more; he called the second boy a blockhead, though really I cannot see why, and passed on to the third, who, for the last minute, had been sitting apparently on hot plates, with his right arm waving up and down like a distracted semaphore signal. He would have had to say it the next second, whether the Professor had asked him or not; he was red in the face, holding his knowledge in.

'A dark and gloomy wood,' shouted the third boy, with much relief to his feelings.

'A dark and gloomy wood,' repeated the Professor, with evident approval. 'And why was it dark and gloomy?'

The third boy was still equal to the occasion.

'Because the sun could not get inside it.'

The Professor felt he had discovered the poet of the class.

'Because the sun could not get into it, or, better, because the sunbeams could not penetrate. And why could not the sunbeams penetrate there?'

'Please, sir, because the leaves were too thick.'

'Very well,' said the Professor. 'The girl lived in a dark and gloomy wood, through the leafy canopy of which the sunbeams were unable to pierce. Now, what grew in this wood?' He pointed to the fourth boy.

'Please, sir, trees, sir.'

'And what else?'

'Toadstools, sir.' This after a pause.

The Professor was not quite sure about the toadstools, but on referring to the text he found that the boy was right; toadstools had been mentioned.

'Quite right,' admitted the Professor, 'toadstools grew there. And what else? What do you find underneath trees in a wood?'

'Please, sir, earth, sir.'

'No; no; what grows in a wood besides trees?'

'Oh please, sir, bushes, sir.'

'Bushes; very good. Now we are getting on. In this wood there were trees and bushes. And what else?'

He pointed to a small boy near the bottom, who having decided that the wood was too far off to be of any annoyance to him, individually, was occupying his leisure playing noughts and crosses against himself. Vexed and bewildered, but feeling it necessary to add something to the inventory, he hazarded blackberries. This was a mistake; the poet had not mentioned blackberries.

'Of course, Klobstock would think of something to eat,' commented the Professor, who prided himself on his ready wit. This raised a laugh against Klobstock, and pleased the Professor.

'You,' continued he, pointing to a boy in the middle; 'what else was there in this wood besides trees and bushes?'

'Please, sir, there was a torrent there.'

'Quite right; and what did the torrent do?'

'Please, sir, it gurgled.'

'No; no. Streams gurgle, torrents——?'

'Roar, sir.'

'It roared. And what made it roar?'

This was a poser. One boy—he was not our prize intellect, I admit—suggested the girl. To help us the Professor put his question in another form:

'When did it roar?'

Our third boy, again coming to the rescue, explained that it roared when it fell down among the rocks. I think some of us had a vague idea that it must have been a cowardly torrent to make such a noise about a little thing like this; a pluckier torrent, we felt, would have got up and gone on, saying nothing about it. A torrent that roared every time it fell upon a rock we deemed a poor spirited torrent; but the Professor seemed quite content with it.

'And what lived in this wood beside the girl?' was the next question.

'Please, sir, birds, sir.'

'Yes, birds lived in this wood. What else?'

Birds seemed to have exhausted our ideas.

'Come,' said the Professor, 'what are those animals with tails, that run up trees?'

We thought for a while, then one of us suggested cats.

This was an error; the poet had said nothing about cats; squirrels was what the Professor was trying to get.

I do not recall much more about this wood in detail. I only recollect that the sky was introduced into it. In places where there occurred an opening among the trees you could by looking up see the sky above you; very often there were clouds in this sky, and occasionally, if I remember rightly, the girl got wet.

I have dwelt upon this incident, because it seems to me suggestive of the whole question of scenery in literature. I could not at the time, I cannot now, understand why the top boy's summary was not sufficient. With all due deference to the poet, whoever he may have been, one cannot but acknowledge that his wood was, and could not be otherwise than, 'the usual sort of a wood.'

I could describe the Black Forest to you at great length. I could translate to you Hebel, the poet of the Black Forest. I could write pages concerning its rocky gorges and its smiling valleys, its pineclad slopes, its rock-crowned summits, its foaming rivulets (where the tidy German has not condemned them to flow respectably through wooden troughs or drain-pipes), its white villages, its lonely farmsteads.

But I am haunted by the suspicion you might skip all this. Were you sufficiently conscientious—or weak-minded enough—not to do so, I should, all said and done, succeed in conveying to you only an impression much better summed up in the simple words of the unpretentious guide-book:

'A picturesque, mountainous district, bounded on the south and the west by the plain of the Rhine, towards which its spurs descend precipitately. Its geological formation consists chiefly of variegated sandstone and granite; its lower heights being covered with extensive pine forests. It is well watered with numerous streams, while its populous valleys are fertile and well cultivated. The inns are good; but the local wines should be partaken of by the stranger with discretion.'

CHAPTER VI

WE arrived at Hamburg on Friday, after a smooth and uneventful voyage; and from Hamburg we travelled to Berlin by way of Hanover. It is not the most direct route. I can only account for our visit to Hanover as the nigger accounted to the magistrate for his appearance in the Deacon's poultry-yard.

'Yes, sar, what the constable sez is quite true, sar; I was dar, sar.'

'Oh, so you admit it? And what were you doing with a sack, pray, in Deacon Abraham's poultry-yard at twelve o'clock at night?'

'I'se gwine ter tell yer, sar; yes, sar. I'd been to Massa Jordan's wid a sack of melons. Yes, sar; an' Massa Jordan he wuz very 'greeable, an' axed me for ter come in.'

'Well?'

'Yes, sar, very 'greeable man is Massa Jordan. An' dar we sat a-talking an' a-talking——'

'Very likely. What we want to know is what you were doing in the Deacon's poultry-yard?'

'Yes, sar, dat's what I'se cumming to. It wuz ver' late 'fore I left Massa Jordan's, an' den I sez ter mysel', sez I, now yer jest step out with yer best leg foremost, Ulysses, case yer gets into trouble wid de old woman. Ver' talkative woman she is, sar, very——'

'Yes, never mind her; there are other people very talkative in this town besides your wife. Deacon Abraham's house is half a mile out of your way home from Mr Jordan's. How did you get there?'

'Dat's what I'm a-gwine ter explain, sar.'

'I am glad of that. And how do you propose to do it?'

'Well, I'se thinkin', sar, I must ha' digressed.'

67

I take it we digressed a little.

At first, from some reason or other, Hanover strikes you as an uninteresting town, but it grows upon you. It is in reality two towns; a place of broad, modern, handsome streets and tasteful gardens; side by side with a sixteenth-century town, where old timbered houses overhang the narrow lanes; where through low archways one catches glimpses of galleried courtyards, once often thronged, no doubt, with troops of horse, or blocked with lumbering coach and six, waiting its rich merchant owner, and his fat placid frau, but where now children and chickens scuttle at their will; while over the carved balconies hang dingy clothes a-drying.

A singularly English atmosphere hovers over Hanover, especially on Sundays, when its shuttered shops and clanging bells give to it the suggestion of a sunnier London. Nor was this British Sunday atmosphere apparent only to myself, else I might have attributed it to imagination; even George felt it. Harris and I, returning from a short stroll with our cigars after lunch on the Sunday afternoon, found him peacefully slumbering in the smoke-room's easiest chair.

'After all,' said Harris, 'there is something about the British Sunday that appeals to the man with English blood in his veins. I should be sorry to see it altogether done away with, let the new generation say what it will.'

And taking one each end of the ample settee, we kept George company.

To Hanover one should go, they say, to learn the best German. The disadvantage is that outside Hanover, which is only a small province, nobody understands this best German. Thus you have to decide whether to speak good German and remain in Hanover, or bad German and travel about. Germany being separated so many centuries into a dozen principalities, is unfortunate in possessing a variety of dialects. Germans from Posen wishful to converse with men of Württemburg, have to talk as often as not in French or English; and young ladies who have received an expensive education in Westphalia surprise and disappoint their parents by being unable to understand a word said to them in Mechlenburg. An English-speaking foreigner, it is true, would find himself equally nonplussed among the Yorkshire wolds, or in the purlieus of Whitechapel; but the cases are not on all fours. Throughout Germany it is not only in the country districts and among the uneducated that dialects are maintained. Every province has practically its own language, of which it is proud and retentive. An educated Bavarian will admit to you that, academically speaking, the North German is more correct; but he will continue to speak South German and to teach it to his children.

In the course of the century, I am inclined to think that Germany will solve her difficulty in this respect by speaking English. Every boy and girl in Germany, above the peasant class, speaks English. Were English pronunciation less arbitrary, there is not the slightest doubt but that in the course of a very few years, comparatively speaking, it would become the language of the world. All foreigners agree that, grammatically, it is the easiest language of any to learn. A German, comparing it with his own language, where every word in every sentence is governed by at least four distinct and separate rules, tells you that English has no grammar. A good many English people would seem to have come to the same conclusion; but they are wrong. As a matter of fact, there is an English grammar, and one of these days our schools will recognize the fact, and it will be taught to our children, penetrating maybe even into literary and journalistic circles. But at present we appear to agree with the foreigner that it is a quantity neglectable. English pronunciation is the stumbling-block to our progress. English spelling would seem to have been designed chiefly as a disguise to pronunciation. It is a clever idea, calculated to check presumption on the part of the foreigner; but for that he would learn it in a year.

For they have a way of teaching languages in Germany that is not our way; and the consequence is that when the German youth or maiden leaves the gymnasium or high school at fifteen, 'it' (as in Germany one conveniently may say) can understand and speak the tongue it has been learning. In England we have a method that for obtaining the least possible result at the greatest possible expenditure of time and money is perhaps unequalled. An English boy who has been through a good middle-class school in England can talk to a Frenchman, slowly and with difficulty, about female gardeners and aunts; conversation which, to a man possessed perhaps of neither, is liable to pall. Possibly, if he be a bright exception, he may be able to tell the time, or make a few guarded observations concerning the weather. No doubt he could repeat a goodly number of irregular verbs by heart; only, as a matter of fact, few foreigners care to listen to their own irregular verbs, recited by young Englishmen. Likewise he

might be able to remember a choice selection of grotesquely
involved French idioms, such as no modern Frenchman has ever
heard or understands when he does hear.

The explanation is that, in nine cases out of ten, he has learnt
French from an 'Ahn's First-Course.' The history of this
famous work is remarkable and instructive. The book was
originally written for a joke by a witty Frenchman who had
resided for some years in England. He intended it as a satire
upon the conversational powers of British society. From this
point of view it was distinctly good. He submitted it to a
London publishing firm. The manager was a shrewd man. He
read the book through. Then he sent for the author.

'This book of yours,' said he to the author, 'is very clever.
I have laughed over it myself till the tears came.'

'I am delighted to hear you say so,' replied the pleased
Frenchman. 'I tried to be truthful without being unnecessarily
offensive.'

'It is most amusing,' concurred the manager; 'and yet published as a harmless joke, I feel it would fail.'

The author's face fell.

'Its humour,' proceeded the manager, 'would be denounced as
forced and extravagant. It would amuse the thoughtful and
intelligent, but from a business point of view that portion of the
public are never worth considering. But I have an idea,' continued the manager. He glanced round the room to be sure they
were alone, and leaning forward sunk his voice to a whisper.
'My notion is to publish it as a serious work for the use of
schools!'

The author stared, speechless.

'I know the English schoolman,' said the manager; 'this book
will appeal to him. It will exactly fit in with his method.
Nothing sillier, nothing more useless for the purpose will he ever
discover. He will smack his lips over the book, as a puppy licks
up blacking.'

The author, sacrificing art to greed, consented. They altered
the title and added a vocabulary, but left the book otherwise as
it was.

The result is known to every schoolboy. 'Ahn' became the
palladium of English philological education. If it no longer
retains its ubiquity, it is because something even less adaptable
to the object in view has been since invented.

Lest, in spite of all, the British schoolboy should obtain, even

from the like of 'Ahn,' some glimmering of French, the British
educational method further handicaps him by bestowing upon
him the assistance of, what is termed in the prospectus, 'A native
gentleman.' This native French gentleman, who, by the by,
is generally a Belgian, is no doubt a most worthy person, and can,
it is true, understand and speak his own language with tolerable
fluency. There his qualifications cease. Invariably he is a man
with a quite remarkable inability to teach anybody anything.
Indeed, he would seem to be chosen not so much as an instructor
as an amuser of youth. He is always a comic figure. No
Frenchman of a dignified appearance would be engaged for any
English school. If he possess by nature a few harmless peculi-
arities, calculated to cause merriment, so much the more is he
esteemed by his employers. The class naturally regards him as
an animated joke. The two to four hours a week that are
deliberately wasted on this ancient farce, are looked forward to by
the boys as a merry interlude in an otherwise monotonous
existence. And then, when the proud parent takes his son and
heir to Dieppe merely to discover that the lad does not know
enough to call a cab, he abuses not the system but its innocent
victim.

I confine my remarks to French, because that is the only language we attempt to teach our youth. An English boy who
could speak German would be looked down upon as unpatriotic.
Why we waste time in teaching even French according to this
method I have never been able to understand. A perfect
unacquaintance with a language is respectable. But putting
aside comic journalists and lady novelists, for whom it is a
business necessity, this smattering of French which we are so
proud to possess only serves to render us ridiculous.

In the German school the method is somewhat different.
One hour every day is devoted to the same language. The idea
is not to give the lad time between each lesson to forget what he
learned at the last; the idea is for him to get on. There is no
comic foreigner provided for his amusement. The desired
language is taught by a German schoolmaster who knows it
inside and out as thoroughly as he knows his own. Maybe this
system does not provide the German youth with that perfection
of foreign accent for which the British tourist is in every land
remarkable, but it has other advantages. The boy does not call
his master 'froggy,' or 'sausage,' nor prepare for the French or
English hour any exhibition of homely wit whatever. He just

sits there, and for his own sake tries to learn that foreign tongue
with as little trouble to everybody concerned as possible.   When
he has left school he can talk, not about penknives and gardeners
and aunts merely, but about European politics, history, Shakespeare, or the musical classes, according to the turn the conversation may take.

Viewing the German people from an Anglo-Saxon standpoint,
it may be that in this book I shall find occasion to criticize them:
but on the other hand, there is much that we might learn from
them; and in the matter of common sense, as applied to education, they can give us ninety-nine in a hundred and beat us with
one hand.

The beautiful wood of the Eilenriede bounds Hanover on the
south and west, and here occurred a sad drama in which Harris
took a prominent part.

We were riding our machines through this wood on the
Monday afternoon in the company of many other cyclists, for it is
a favourite resort with the Hanoverians on a sunny afternoon,
and its shady pathways are then filled with happy, thoughtless
folk.   Among them rode a young and beautiful girl on a machine
that was new.   She was evidently a novice on the bicycle.   One
felt instinctively that there would come a moment when she
would require help, and Harris, with his accustomed chivalry,
suggested we should keep near her.   Harris, as he occasionally
explains to George and to myself, has daughters of his own, or, to
speak more correctly, a daughter, who as the years progress will
no doubt cease practising catherine wheels in the front garden,
and will grow up into a beautiful and respectable young lady.
This naturally gives Harris an interest in all beautiful girls up to
the age of thirty-five or thereabouts; they remind him, so he says,
of home.

We had ridden for about two miles, when we noticed, a little
ahead of us in a space where five ways met, a man with a hose,
watering the roads.   The pipe, supported at each joint by a pair
of tiny wheels, writhed after him as he moved, suggesting a
gigantic worm, from whose open neck, as the man, gripping it
firmly in both hands, pointing it now this way, and now that,
now elevating it, now depressing it, poured a strong stream of
water at the rate of about a gallon a second.

'What a much better method than ours,' observed Harris
enthusiastically.   Harris is inclined to be chronically severe on
all British institutions.   'How much simpler, quicker, and more

economical! You see, one man by this method can in five minutes water a stretch of road that would take us with our clumsy lumbering cart half an hour to cover.'

George, who was riding behind me on the tandem, said: 'Yes, and it is also a method by which with a little carelessness a man could cover a good many people in a good deal less time than they could get out of the way.'

George, the opposite to Harris, is British to the core. I remember George quite patriotically indignant with Harris once for suggesting the introduction of the guillotine into England.

'It is so much neater,' said Harris.

'I don't care if it is,' said George; 'I'm an Englishman; hanging is good enough for me.'

'Our water-cart may have its disadvantages,' continued George, 'but it can only make you uncomfortable about the legs, and you can avoid it. This is the sort of machine with which a man can follow you round the corner and upstairs.'

'It fascinates me to watch them,' said Harris. 'They are so skilful. I have seen a man from the corner of a crowded square in Strassburg cover every inch of ground, and not so much as wet an apron string. It is marvellous how they judge their distance. They will send the water up to your toes, and then bring it over your head so that it falls around your heels. They can——'

'Ease up a minute,' said George.

I said: 'Why?'

He said: 'I am going to get off and watch the rest of this show from behind a tree. There may be great performers in this line, as Harris says; this particular artist appears to me to lack something. He has just soused a dog, and now he's busy watering a signpost. I am going to wait till he has finished.'

'Nonsense,' said Harris; 'he won't wet you.'

'That is precisely what I am going to make sure of,' answered George, saying which he jumped off, and, taking up a position behind a remarkably fine elm, pulled out and commenced filling his pipe.

I did not care to take the tandem on by myself, so I stepped off and joined him, leaving the machine against a tree. Harris shouted something or other about our being a disgrace to the land that gave us birth, and rode on.

The next moment I heard a woman's cry of distress. Glancing round the stem of the tree, I perceived that it proceeded from the young and elegant lady before mentioned, whom, in our interest concerning the road-waterer, we had forgotten. She was riding her machine steadily and straightly through a drenching shower of water from the hose. She appeared to be too paralysed either to get off or turn her wheel aside. Every instant she was becoming wetter, while the man with the hose, who was either drunk or blind, continued to pour water upon her with utter indifference. A dozen voices yelled imprecations upon him, but he took no heed whatever.

Harris, his fatherly nature stirred to its depths, did at this point what, under the circumstances, was quite the right and proper thing to do. Had he acted throughout with the same coolness and judgment he then displayed, he would have emerged from that incident the hero of the hour, instead of, as happened, riding away followed by insult and threat. Without a moment's hesitation he spurted at the man, sprang to the ground, and, seizing the hose by the nozzle, attempted to wrest it away.

What he ought to have done, what any man retaining his common sense would have done the moment he got his hands upon the thing, was to turn off the tap. Then he might have played football with the man, or battledore and shuttlecock as he pleased; and the twenty or thirty people who had rushed forward to assist would have only applauded. His idea, however, as he explained to us afterwards, was to take away the hose from the man, and, for punishment, turn it upon the fool himself. The waterman's idea appeared to be the same, namely, to retain the hose as a weapon with which to soak Harris. Of course, the result was that, between them, they soused every dead and living thing within fifty yards, except themselves. One furious man, too drenched to care what more happened to him, leapt into the arena and also took a hand. The three among them proceeded to sweep the compass with that hose. They pointed it to heaven, and the water descended upon the people in the form of an equinoctial storm. They pointed it downwards, and sent the water in rushing streams that took people off their feet, or caught them about the waist line, and doubled them up.

Not one of them would loosen his grip upon the hose, not one of them thought to turn the water off. You might have concluded they were struggling with some primeval force of nature. In forty-five seconds, so George said, who was timing it, they had swept that circus bare of every living thing except one dog, who, dripping like a water nymph, rolled over by the force of water,

now on this side, now on that, still gallantly staggered again and
again to its feet to bark defiance at what it evidently regarded as
the powers of hell let loose.

Men and women left their machines upon the ground, and flew
into the woods. From behind every tree of importance peeped
out wet, angry heads.

At last, there arrived upon the scene one man of sense.
Braving all things, he crept to the hydrant, where still stood the
iron key, and screwed it down. And then from forty trees began
to creep more or less soaked human beings, each one with something to say.

At first I fell to wondering whether a stretcher or a clothes-
basket would be the more useful for the conveyance of Harris's
remains back to the hotel. I consider that George's promptness
on that occasion saved Harris's life. Being dry, and therefore
able to run quicker, he was there before the crowd. Harris was
for explaining things, but George cut him short.

'You get on that,' said George, handing him his bicycle, 'and
go. They don't know we belong to you, and you may trust us
implicitly not to reveal the secret. We'll hang about behind, and
get in their way. Ride zigzag in case they shoot.'

I wish this book to be a strict record of fact, unmarred by
exaggeration, and therefore I have shown my description of this
incident to Harris, lest anything beyond bald narrative may have
crept into it. Harris maintains it is exaggerated, but admits that
one or two people may have been 'sprinkled.' I have offered to
turn a street hose on him at a distance of five-and-twenty yards,
and take his opinion afterwards, as to whether 'sprinkled' is the
adequate term, but he has declined the test. Again, he insists
there could not have been more than half a dozen people, at the
outside, involved in the catastrophe, that forty is a ridiculous
mis-statement. I have offered to return with him to Hanover
and make strict inquiry into the matter, and this offer he has
likewise declined. Under these circumstances, I maintain that
mine is a true and restrained narrative of an event that is, by a
certain number of Hanoverians, remembered with bitterness
unto this very day.

We left Hanover that same evening, and arrived at Berlin in
time for supper and an evening stroll. Berlin is a disappointing
town; its centre overcrowded, its outlying parts lifeless, its one
famous street, Unter den Linden, an attempt to combine Oxford
Street with the Champs Elysée, singularly unimposing, being

much too wide for its size; its theatres dainty and charming, where acting is considered of more importance than scenery or dress, where long runs are unknown, successful pieces being played again and again, but never consecutively, so that for a week running you may go to the same Berlin theatre and see a fresh play every night; its opera house unworthy of it; its two music halls, with an unnecessary suggestion of vulgarity and commonness about them, ill-arranged and much too large for comfort. In the Berlin cafés and restaurants, the busy time is from midnight on till three. Yet most of the people who frequent them are up again at seven. Either the Berliner has solved the great problem of modern life: how to do without sleep, or, with Carlyle, he must be looking forward to eternity.

Personally, I know of no other town where such late hours are the vogue, except St Petersburg. But your St Petersburger does not get up early in the morning. At St Petersburg, the music halls, which it is the fashionable thing to attend *after* the theatre —a drive to them taking half an hour in a swift sleigh—do not practically begin till twelve. Through the Neva at four o'clock in the morning you have to literally push your way; and the favourite trains for travellers are those starting about five o'clock in the morning. These trains save the Russian the trouble of getting up early. He wishes his friends 'Good night,' and drives down to the station comfortably after supper, without putting the house to any inconvenience.

Potsdam, the Versailles to Berlin, is a beautiful little town, situate among lakes and woods. Here in the shady ways of its quiet, far-stretching park of Sans Souci, it is easy to imagine lean, snuffy Frederick 'bummeling' with shrill Voltaire.

Acting on my advice, George and Harris consented not to stay long in Berlin, but to push on to Dresden. Most that Berlin has to show can be seen better elsewhere, and we decided to be content with a drive through the town. The hotel porter introduced us to a droshky driver, under whose guidance, so he assured us, we should see everything worth seeing in the shortest possible time. The man himself, who called for us at nine o'clock in the morning, was all that could be desired. He was bright, intelligent, and well-informed; his German was easy to understand and he knew a little English with which to eke it out on occasion. With the man himself there was no fault to be found, but his horse was the most unsympathetic brute I have ever sat behind.

He took a dislike to us the moment he saw us. I was the first to come out of the hotel. He turned his head, and looked me up and down with a cold, glassy eye; and then he looked across at another horse, a friend of his that was standing facing him. I knew what he said. He had an expressive head, and he made no attempt to disguise his thought. He said:

'Funny things one does come across in the summer time, don't one?'

George followed me out the next moment, and stood behind me. The horse again turned his head and looked. I have never known a horse that could twist himself as this horse did. I have seen a camelopard do tricks with his neck that compelled one's attention, but this animal was more like the thing one dreams of after a dusty day at Ascot, followed by a dinner with six old chums. If I had seen his eyes looking at me from between his own hind legs, I doubt if I should have been surprised. He seemed more amused with George, if anything, than with myself. He turned to his friend again.

'Extraordinary, isn't it?' he remarked; 'I suppose there must be some place where they grow them'; and then he commenced licking flies off his own left shoulder. I began to wonder whether he had lost his mother when young, and had been brought up by a cat.

George and I climbed in, and sat waiting for Harris. He came a moment later. Myself, I thought he looked rather neat. He wore a white flannel knickerbocker suit, which he had had made specially for bicycling in hot weather; his hat may have been a trifle out of the common, but it did keep the sun off.

The horse gave one look at him, said 'Gott in Himmel!' as plainly as ever horse spoke, and started off down Friedrich Strasse at a brisk walk, leaving Harris and the driver standing on the pavement. His owner called to him to stop, but he took no notice. They ran after us, and overtook us at the corner of the Dorotheen Strasse. I could not catch what the man said to the horse, he spoke quickly and excitedly; but I gathered a few phrases, such as:

'Got to earn my living somehow, haven't I?' 'Who asked for your opinion?' 'Aye, little you care so long as you can guzzle.'

The horse cut the conversation short by turning up the Dorotheen Strasse on his own account. I think what he said was:

'Come on then; don't talk so much. Let's get the job over, and, where possible, let's keep to the back streets.'

Opposite the Brandenburger Thor our driver hitched the reins to the whip, climbed down, and came round to explain things to us. He pointed out the Thiergarten, and then descanted to us of the Reichstag House. He informed us of its exact height, length, and breadth, after the manner of guides. Then he turned his attention to the Gate. He said it was constructed of sandstone, in imitation of the 'Properleer' in Athens.

At this point the horse, which had been occupying its leisure licking its own legs, turned round its head. It did not say anything, it just looked.

The man began again nervously. This time he said it was an imitation of the 'Propeyedliar.'

Here the horse proceeded up the Linden, and nothing would persuade him not to proceed up the Linden. His owner expostulated with him, but he continued to trot on. From the way he hitched his shoulders as he moved, I somehow felt he was saying:

'They've seen the Gate, haven't they? Very well, that's enough. As for the rest, you don't know what you are talking about, and they wouldn't understand you if you did. You talk German.'

It was the same throughout the length of the Linden. The horse consented to stand still sufficiently long to enable us to have a good look at each sight, and to hear the name of it. All explanation and description he cut short by the simple process of moving on.

'What these fellows want,' he seemed to say to himself, 'is to go home and tell people they have seen these things. If I am doing them an injustice, if they are more intelligent than they look, they can get better information than this old fool of mine is giving them from the guide-book. Who wants to know how high a steeple is? You don't remember it the next five minutes when you are told, and if you do it is because you have nothing else in your head. He just tires me with his talk. Why doesn't he hurry up, and let us all get home to lunch?'

Upon reflection, I am not sure that wall-eyed old brute had not sense on its side. Anyhow, I know there have been occasions, with a guide, when I would have been glad of its interference.

But one is apt to 'sin one's mercies,' as the Scotch say, and at the time we cursed that horse instead of blessing it.

CHAPTER VII

At a point between Berlin and Dresden, George, who had, for
the last quarter of an hour or so, been looking very attentively
out of the window, said:

'Why, in Germany, is it the custom to put the letter-box up a
tree? Why do they not fix it to the front door as we do? I
should hate having to climb up a tree to get my letters. Besides,
it is not fair to the postman. In addition to being most exhausting, the delivery of letters must to a heavy man, on windy
nights, be positively dangerous work. If they will fix it to a
tree, why not fix it lower down, why always among the topmost
branches? But, maybe, I am misjudging the country,' he continued, a new idea occurring to him. 'Possibly the Germans,
who are in many matters ahead of us, have perfected a pigeon
post. Even so, I cannot help thinking they would have been
wiser to train the birds, while they were about it, to deliver the
letters nearer the ground. Getting your letters out of those
boxes must be tricky work even to the average middle-aged
German.'

I followed his gaze out of window. I said:

'Those are not letter-boxes, they are birds' nests. You must
understand this nation. The German loves birds, but he likes
tidy birds. A bird left to himself builds his nest just anywhere.
It is not a pretty object, according to the German notion of
prettiness. There is not a bit of paint on it anywhere, not a
plaster image all round, not even a flag. The nest finished, the
bird proceeds to live outside it. He drops things on the grass;
twigs, ends of worms, all sorts of things. He is indelicate. He
makes love, quarrels with his wife, and feeds the children quite

79

in public. The German householder is shocked. He says to
the bird:

"'For many things I like you. I like to look at you. I like to
hear you sing. But I don't like your ways. Take this little box,
and put your rubbish inside where I can't see it. Come out
when you want to sing; but let your domestic arrangements be
confined to the interior. Keep to the box, and don't make the
garden untidy.'"

In Germany one breathes in love of order with the air, in
Germany the babies beat time with their rattles, and the German
bird has come to prefer the box, and to regard with contempt the
few uncivilized outcasts who continue to build their nests in trees
and hedges. In course of time every German bird, one is confident, will have his proper place in a full chorus. This promis-
cuous and desultory warbling of his must, one feels, be irritating
to the precise German mind; there is no method in it. The
music-loving German will organize him. Some stout bird with
a specially well-developed crop will be trained to conduct him,
and, instead of wasting himself in a wood at four o'clock in the
morning, he will, at the advertised time, sing in a beer garden,
accompanied by a piano. Things are drifting that way.

Your German likes nature, but his idea of nature is a glorified
Welsh Harp. He takes great interest in his garden. He plants
seven rose trees on the north side and seven on the south, and if
they do not grow up all the same size and shape it worries him so
that he cannot sleep of nights. Every flower he ties to a stick.
This interferes with his view of the flower, but he has the satisfaction of knowing it is there, and that it is behaving itself. The
lake is lined with zinc, and once a week he takes it up, carries it
into the kitchen, and scours it. In the geometrical centre of the
grass plot, which is sometimes as large as a tablecloth, and is
generally railed round, he places a china dog. The Germans are
very fond of dogs, but as a rule they prefer them of china. The
china dog never digs holes in the lawn to bury bones, and never
scatters a flower-bed to the winds with his hind legs. From the
German point of view, he is the ideal dog. He stops where you
put him, and he is never where you do not want him. You can
have him perfect in all points, according to the latest require-
ments of the Kennel Club; or you can indulge your own fancy
and have something unique. You are not, as with other dogs,
limited to breed. In china, you can have a blue dog or a pink
dog. For a little extra, you can have a double-headed dog.

On a certain fixed date in the autumn the German stakes his flowers and bushes to the earth, and covers them with Chinese matting; and on a certain fixed date in the spring he uncovers them, and stands them up again.   If it happens to be an exceptionally fine autumn, or an exceptionally late spring, so much the worse for the unfortunate vegetable.   No true German would allow his arrangements to be interfered with by so unruly a thing as the solar system.   Unable to regulate the weather, he ignores it.

Among trees, your German's favourite is the poplar.   Other disorderly nations may sing the charms of the rugged oak, the spreading chestnut, or the waving elm.   To the German all such, with their wilful, untidy ways, are eyesores.   The poplar grows where it is planted, and how it is planted.   It has no improper rugged ideas of its own.   It does not want to wave or to spread itself.   It just grows straight and upright as a German tree should grow; and so gradually the German is rooting out all other trees, and replacing them with poplars.

Your German likes the country, but he prefers it as the lady thought she would the noble savage—more dressed.   He likes his walk through the wood—to a restaurant.   But the pathway must not be too steep, it must have a brick gutter running down one side of it to drain it, and every twenty yards or so it must have its seat on which he can rest and mop his brow; for your German would no more think of sitting on the grass than would an English bishop dream of rolling down One Tree Hill.   He likes his view from the summit of the hill, but he likes to find there a stone tablet telling him what to look at, and a table and bench at which he can sit to partake of the frugal beer and *belegte Semmel* he has been careful to bring with him.   If, in addition, he can find a police notice posted on a tree, forbidding him to do something or other, that gives him an extra sense of comfort and security.

Your German is not averse even to wild scenery, provided it be not too wild.   But if he consider it too savage, he sets to work to tame it.   I remember, in the neighbourhood of Dresden, discovering a picturesque and narrow valley leading down towards the Elbe.   The winding roadway ran beside a mountain torrent, which for a mile or so fretted and foamed over rocks and boulders between wood-covered banks.   I followed it enchanted until, turning a corner, I suddenly came across a gang of eighty or a hundred workmen.   They were busy tidying up that valley, and making that stream respectable. All the stones that were impeding the course of the water they were carefully picking out and carting away. The bank on either side they were bricking up and cementing. The overhanging trees and bushes, the tangled vines and creepers they were rooting up and trimming down. A little farther I came upon the finished work—the mountain valley as it ought to be, according to German ideas. The water, now a broad, sluggish stream, flowed over a level, gravelly bed, between two walls, crowned with stone coping. At every hundred yards it gently descended down three shallow wooden platforms. For a space on either side the ground had been cleared, and at regular intervals young poplars planted. Each sapling was protected by a shield of wickerwork and bossed by an iron rod. In the course of a couple of years it is the hope of the local council to have 'finished' that valley throughout its entire length, and made it fit for a tidy-minded lover of German nature to walk in. There will be a seat every fifty yards, a police notice every hundred, and a restaurant every half-mile.

They are doing the same from the Memel to the Rhine. They are just tidying up the country. I remember well the Wehrthal. It was once the most romantic ravine to be found in the Black Forest. The last time I walked down it some hundreds of Italian workmen were encamped there hard at work, training the wild little Wehr the way it should go, bricking the banks for it here, blasting the rocks for it there, making cement steps for it down which it can travel soberly and without fuss.

For in Germany there is no nonsense talked about untrammelled nature. In Germany nature has got to behave herself, and not set a bad example to the children. A German poet, noticing waters coming down as Southey describes, somewhat inexactly, the waters coming down at Lodore, would be too shocked to stop and write alliterative verse about them. He would hurry away, and at once report them to the police. Then their foaming and their shrieking would be of short duration.

'Now then, now then, what's all this about?' the voice of German authority would say severely to the waters. 'We can't have this sort of thing, you know. Come down quietly, can't you? Where do you think you are?'

And the local German council would provide those waters with zinc pipes and wooden troughs, and a corkscrew staircase, and show them how to come down sensibly, in the German manner.

It is a tidy land is Germany.

We reached Dresden on the Wednesday evening, and stayed there over the Sunday.

Taking one consideration with another, Dresden, perhaps, is the most attractive town in Germany; but it is a place to be lived in for a while rather than visited. Its museums and galleries, its palaces and gardens, its beautiful and historically rich environment, provide pleasure for a winter, but bewilder for a week. It has not the gaiety of Paris or Vienna, which quickly palls; its charms are more solidly German, and more lasting. It is the Mecca of the musician. For five shillings, in Dresden, you can purchase a stall at the opera house, together, unfortunately, with a strong disinclination ever again to take the trouble of sitting out a performance in any English, French, or American opera house.

The chief scandal of Dresden still centres round August the Strong, 'the Man of Sin,' as Carlyle always called him, who is popularly reputed to have cursed Europe with over a thousand children. Castles where he imprisoned this discarded mistress or that—one of them, who persisted in her claim to a better title, for forty years, it is said, poor lady! The narrow rooms where she ate her heart out and died are still shown. Châteaux, shameful for this deed of infamy or that, lie scattered round the neighbourhood like bones about a battlefield; and most of your guide's stories are such as the 'young person' educated in Germany had best not hear. His life-sized portrait hangs in the fine Zwinger, which he built as an arena for his wild beast fights when the people grew tired of them in the market-place; a beetle-browed, frankly animal man, but with the culture and taste that so often wait upon animalism. Modern Dresden undoubtedly owes much to him.

But what the stranger in Dresden stares at most is, perhaps, its electric trams. These huge vehicles flash through the streets at from ten to twenty miles an hour, taking curves and corners after the manner of an Irish car driver. Everybody travels by them, excepting only officers in uniform, who must not. Ladies in evening dress, going to ball or opera, porters with their baskets, sit side by side. They are all-important in the streets, and everything and everybody makes haste to get out of their way. If you do not get out of their way, and you still happen to be alive when picked up, then on your recovery you are fined for having been in their way. This teaches you to be wary of them.

One afternoon Harris took a 'bummel' by himself. In the

evening, as we sat listening to the band at the Belvedere, Harris said, a propos of nothing in particular: 'These Germans have no sense of humour.'

'What makes you think that?' I asked.

'Why, this afternoon,' he answered, 'I jumped on one of those electric tramcars. I wanted to see the town, so I stood outside on the little platform—what do you call it?'

'The Stehplatz,' I suggested.

'That's it,' said Harris. 'Well, you know the way they shake you about, and how you have to look out for the corners, and mind yourself when they stop and when they start?'

I nodded.

'There were about half a dozen of us standing there,' he continued, 'and, of course, I am not experienced. The thing started suddenly, and that jerked me backwards. I fell against a stout gentleman, just behind me. He could not have been standing very firmly himself, and he, in his turn, fell back against a boy who was carrying a trumpet in a green baize case. They never smiled, neither the man nor the boy with the trumpet; they just stood there and looked sulky. I was going to say I was sorry, but before I could get the words out the tram eased up, for some reason or other, and that, of course, shot me forward again, and I butted into a white-haired old chap, who looked to me like a professor. Well, *he* never smiled, never moved a muscle.'

'Maybe, he was thinking of something else,' I suggested.

'That could not have been the case with them all,' replied Harris, 'and in the course of that journey, I must have fallen against every one of them at least three times. You see,' explained Harris, 'they knew when the corners were coming, and in which direction to brace themselves. I, as a stranger, was naturally at a disadvantage. The way I rolled and staggered about that platform, clutching wildly now at this man and now at that, must have been really comic. I don't say it was high-class humour, but it would have amused most people. Those Germans seemed to see no fun in it whatever—just seemed anxious, that was all. There was one man, a little man, who stood with his back against the brake; I fell against him five times, I counted them. You would have expected the fifth time would have dragged a laugh out of him, but it didn't; he merely looked tired. They are a dull lot.'

George also had an adventure at Dresden. There was a shop

near the Altmarkt, in the window of which were exhibited some cushions for sale. The proper business of the shop was handling of glass and china; the cushions appeared to be in the nature of an experiment. They were very beautiful cushions, hand-embroidered on satin. We often passed the shop, and every time George paused and examined those cushions. He said he thought his aunt would like one.

George has been very attentive to this aunt of his during the journey. He has written her quite a long letter every day, and from every town we stop at he sends her off a present. To my mind, he is overdoing the business, and more than once I have expostulated with him. His aunt will be meeting other aunts, and talking to them; the whole class will become disorganized and unruly. As a nephew, I object to the impossible standard that George is setting up. But he will not listen.

Therefore it was that on the Saturday he left us after lunch, saying he would go round to that shop and get one of those cushions for his aunt. He said he would not be long, and suggested our waiting for him.

We waited for what seemed to me rather a long time. When he rejoined us he was empty handed, and looked worried. We asked him where his cushion was. He said he hadn't got a cushion, said he had changed his mind, said he didn't think his aunt would care for a cushion. Evidently something was amiss. We tried to get at the bottom of it, but he was not communicative. Indeed, his answers after our twentieth question or thereabouts became quite short.

In the evening, however, when he and I happened to be alone, he broached the subject himself. He said:

'They are somewhat peculiar in some things, these Germans.'

I said: 'What has happened?'

'Well,' he answered, 'there was that cushion I wanted.'

'For your aunt,' I remarked.

'Why not?' he returned. He was huffy in a moment; I never knew a man so touchy about an aunt. 'Why shouldn't I send a cushion to my aunt?'

'Don't get excited,' I replied. 'I am not objecting; I respect you for it.'

He recovered his temper, and went on:

'There were four in the window, if you remember, all very much alike, and each one labelled in plain figures twenty marks. I don't pretend to speak German fluently, but I can generally make myself understood with a little effort, and gather the sense of what is said to me, provided they don't gabble. I went into the shop. A young girl came up to me; she was a pretty, quiet little soul, one might almost say, demure; not at all the sort of girl from whom you would have expected such a thing. I was never more surprised in all my life.'

'Surprised about what?' I said.

George always assumes you know the end of the story while he is telling you the beginning; it is an annoying method.

'At what happened,' replied George; 'at what I am telling you. She smiled and asked me what I wanted. I understood that all right; there could have been no mistake about that. I put down a twenty-mark piece on the counter and said:

'"Please give me a cushion."

'She stared at me as if I had asked for a feather-bed. I thought, maybe she had not heard, so I repeated it louder. If I had chucked her under the chin she could not have looked more surprised or indignant.

'She said she thought I must be making a mistake.

'I did not want to begin a long conversation and find myself stranded. I said there was no mistake. I pointed to my twenty-mark piece, and repeated for the third time that I wanted a cushion, "a twenty-mark cushion."

'Another girl came up, an elder girl; and the first girl repeated to her what I had just said: she seemed quite excited about it. The second girl did not believe her—did not think I looked the sort of man who would want a cushion. To make sure, she put the question to me herself.

'"Did you say you wanted a cushion?" she asked.

'"I have said it three times," I answered. "I will say it again —I want a cushion."

'She said: "Then you can't have one."

'I was getting angry by this time. If I hadn't really wanted the thing I should have walked out of the shop; but there the cushions were in the window, evidently for sale. I didn't see *why* I couldn't have one.

'I said: "I will have one!" It is a simple sentence. I said it with determination.

'A third girl came up at this point, the three representing, I fancy, the whole force of the shop. She was a bright-eyed, saucy-looking little wench, this last one. On any other occasion I might have been pleased to see her; now, her coming only irritated me. I didn't see the need of three girls for this business.

'The first two girls started explaining the thing to the third girl, and before they were half-way through, the third girl began to giggle—she was the sort of girl who would giggle at anything. That done, they fell to chattering like Jenny Wrens, all three together; and between every half-dozen words they looked across at me; and the more they looked at me the more the third girl giggled; and before they had finished they were all three giggling, the little idiots; you might have thought I was a clown, giving a private performance.

'When she was steady enough to move, the third girl came up to me; she was still giggling. She said:

'"If you get it, will you go?"

'I did not quite understand her at first, and she repeated it.

'"This cushion. When you've got it, will you go—away—at once?"

'I was only too anxious to go. I told her so. But, I added I was not going without it. I had made up my mind to have that cushion now if I stopped in the shop all night for it.

'She rejoined the other two girls. I thought they were going to get me the cushion and have done with the business. Instead of that, the strangest thing possible happened. The two other girls got behind the first girl, all three still giggling, heaven knows what about, and pushed her towards me. They pushed her close up to me, and then, before I knew what was happening, she put her hands on my shoulders, stood up on tiptoe, and kissed me. After which, burying her face in her apron, she ran off, followed by the second girl. The third girl opened the door for me, and so evidently expected me to go, that in my confusion I went, leaving my twenty marks behind me. I don't say I minded the kiss, though I did not particularly want it, while I did want the cushion. I don't like to go back to the shop. I cannot understtand the thing at all.'

I said: 'What did you ask for?'

He said: 'A cushion.'

I said: 'That is what you wanted, I know. What I mean is, what was the actual German word you said?'

He replied: 'A *kuss*.'

I said: 'You have nothing to complain of. It is somewhat confusing. A *kuss* sounds as if it ought to be a cushion, but it is not; it is a kiss, while a *kissen* is a cushion. You muddled up the two words—people have done it before. I don't know much about this sort of thing myself; but you asked for a twenty-mark kiss, and from your description of the girl some people might consider the price reasonable. Anyhow, I should not tell Harris. If I remember rightly, he also has an aunt.'

George agreed with me it would be better not.

CHAPTER VIII

Mr and Miss Jones, of Manchester—The benefits of cocoa—A hint to the Peace Society—The window as a medieval argument—The favourite Christian recreation—The language of the guide—How to repair the ravages of time—George tries a bottle—The fate of the German beer drinker—Harris and I resolve to do a good action—The usual sort of statue—Harris and his friends—A pepperless Paradise—Women and towns.

WE were on our way to Prague, and were waiting in the great hall of the Dresden station until such time as the powers-that-be should permit us on to the platform. George, who had wandered to the bookstall, returned to us with a wild look in his eyes. He said:

'I've seen it.'

I said: 'Seen what?'

He was too excited to answer intelligently. He said:

'It's here. It's coming this way, both of them. If you wait, you'll see it for yourselves. I'm not joking; it's the real thing.'

As is usual about this period, some paragraphs, more or less serious, had been appearing in the papers concerning the sea-serpent, and I thought for the moment he must be referring to this. A moment's reflection, however, told me that here, in the middle of Europe, three hundred miles from the coast, such a thing was impossible. Before I could question him further, he seized me by the arm.

'Look!' he said; 'now am I exaggerating?'

I turned my head and saw what, I suppose, few living Englishmen have ever seen before—the travelling Britisher according to the Continental idea, accompanied by his daughter. They were coming towards us in the flesh and blood, unless we were dreaming, alive and concrete—the English 'Milor' and the English 'Mees,' as for generations they have been portrayed in the Continental comic press and upon the Continental stage. They were perfect in every detail. The man was tall and thin, with sandy hair, a huge nose, and long Dundreary whiskers. Over a pepper-and-salt suit he wore a light overcoat, reaching almost to his heels. His white helmet was ornamented with a green veil;

a pair of opera-glasses hung at his side, and in his lavender-gloved hand he carried an alpenstock a little taller than himself. His daughter was long and angular. Her dress I cannot describe: my grandfather, poor gentleman, might have been able to do so; it would have been more familiar to him. I can only say that it appeared to me unnecessarily short, exhibiting a pair of ankles—if I may be permitted to refer to such points—that, from an artistic point of view, called rather for concealment. Her hat made me think of Mrs Hemans; but why I cannot explain. She wore side-spring boots—'prunella,' I believe, used to be the trade name—mittens, and pince-nez. She also carried an alpenstock (there is not a mountain within a hundred miles of Dresden) and a black bag strapped to her waist. Her teeth stuck out like a rabbit's, and her figure was that of a bolster on stilts.

Harris rushed for his camera, and of course could not find it; he never can when he wants it. Whenever we see Harris scuttling up and down like a lost dog, shouting: 'Where's my camera? What the dickens have I done with my camera? Don't either of you remember where I put my camera?'—then we know that for the first time that day he has come across something worth photographing. Later on, he remembered it was in his bag; that is where it would be on an occasion like this.

They were not content with appearance; they acted the thing to the letter. They walked gaping round them at every step. The gentleman had an open Baedeker in his hand, and the lady carried a phrase-book. They talked French that nobody could understand, and German that they could not translate themselves! The man poked at officials with his alpenstock to attract their attention, and the lady, her eye catching sight of an advertisement of somebody's cocoa, said 'Shocking!' and turned the other way.

Really, there was some excuse for her. One notices, even in England, the home of the proprieties, that the lady who drinks cocoa appears, according to the poster, to require very little else in this world; a yard or so of art muslin at the most. On the Continent, she dispenses, so far as one can judge, with every other necessity of life. Not only is cocoa food and drink to her, it should be clothes also, according to the idea of the cocoa manufacturer. But this by the way.

Of course, they immediately became the centre of attraction. By being able to render them some slight assistance, I gained the advantage of five minutes' conversation with them. They were

THREE MEN ON THE BUMMEL 91

very affable. The gentleman told me his name was Jones, and
that he came from Manchester, but he did not seem to know
what part of Manchester, or where Manchester was. I asked
him where he was going to, but he evidently did not know. He
said it depended. I asked him if he did not find an alpenstock a
clumsy thing to walk about with through a crowded town; he
admitted that occasionally it did get in the way. I asked him if
he did not find a veil interfere with his view of things; he explained that you only wore it when the flies became troublesome.
I inquired of the lady if she did not find the wind blow cold; she
said she had noticed it, especially at the corners. I did not ask
these questions one after another as I have here put them down;
I mixed them up with general conversation, and we parted on
good terms.

I have pondered much upon the apparition, and have come to
a definite opinion. A man I met later at Frankfort, and to whom
I described the pair, said he had seen them himself in Paris, three
weeks after the termination of the Fashoda incident; while a
traveller for some English steel works whom we met in Strassburg remembered having seen them in Berlin during the excitement caused by the Transvaal question. My conclusion is that
they were actors out of work, hired to do this thing in the interest
of international peace. The French Foreign Office, wishful to
allay the anger of the Parisian mob clamouring for war with
England, secured this admirable couple and sent them round the
town. You cannot be amused at a thing and at the same time
want to kill it. The French nation saw the English citizen and
citizeness—no caricature, but the living reality—and their
indignation exploded in laughter. The success of the stratagem
prompted them later on to offer their services to the German
Government, with the beneficial results that we all know.

Our own Government might learn the lesson. It might be as
well to keep near Downing Street a few small, fat Frenchmen, to
be sent round the country when occasion called for it, shrugging
their shoulders and eating frog sandwiches; or a file of untidy,
lank-haired Germans might be retained, to walk about, smoking
long pipes, saying 'So.' The public would laugh and exclaim:
'War with such? It would be too absurd.' Failing the
Government, I recommend the scheme to the Peace Society.

Our visit to Prague we were compelled to lengthen somewhat.
Prague is one of the most interesting towns in Europe. Its
stones are saturated with history and romance; its every suburb

must have been a battlefield.   It is the town that conceived the
Reformation and hatched the Thirty Years War. But half
Prague's troubles, one imagines, might have been saved to it, had
it possessed windows less large and temptingly convenient.
The first of these mighty catastrophes it set rolling by throwing
the seven Catholic councillors from the windows of its Rathhaus
on to the pikes of the Hussites below.   Later, it gave the signal
for the second by again throwing the Imperial councillors from
the windows of the old Burg in the Hradschin—Prague's second
'Fenstersturz.'   Since, other fateful questions have been decided
in Prague; one assumes from their having been concluded
without violence that such must have been discussed in cellars.
The window, as an argument, one feels, would always have
proved too strong a temptation to any true-born Praguer.

In the Teynkirche stands the wormeaten pulpit from which
preached John Huss.   One may hear from the selfsame desk
to-day the voice of a Papist priest, while in far-off Constance a
rude block of stone, half ivy hidden, marks the spot where Huss
and Jerome died burning at the stake.   History is fond of her
little ironies.   In this same Teynkirche lies buried Tycho Brahe,
the astronomer, who made the common mistake of thinking the
earth, with its eleven hundred creeds and one humanity, the
centre of the universe; but who otherwise observed the stars
clearly.

Through Prague's dirty, palace-bordered alleys must have
pressed often in hot haste blind Ziska and open-minded Wallen-
stein—they have dubbed him 'The Hero' in Prague; and the
town is honestly proud of having owned him for citizen.   In his
gloomy palace in the Waldstein-Platz they show as a sacred spot
the cabinet where he prayed, and seem to have persuaded themselves he really had a soul.   Its steep, winding ways must have
been choked a dozen times, now by Sigismund's flying legions,
followed by fierce-killing Tarborites, and now by pale Protes-
tants pursued by the victorious Catholics of Maximilian.   Now
Saxons, now Bavarians, and now French; now the saints of
Gustavus Adolphus, and now the steel fighting machines of
Frederick the Great, have thundered at its gates and fought upon
its bridges.

The Jews have always been an important feature of Prague.
Occasionally they have assisted the Christians in their favourite
occupation of slaughtering one another, and the great flag sus-
pended from the vaulting of the Altneuschule testifies to the

courage with which they helped Catholic Ferdinand to resist the Protestant Swedes. The Prague Ghetto was one of the first to be established in Europe, and in the tiny synagogue, still standing, the Jew of Prague has worshipped for eight hundred years, his womenfolk devoutly listening, without, at the ear holes provided for them in the massive walls. A Jewish cemetery adjacent, 'Bethchajim, or the House of Life,' seems as though it were bursting with its dead. Within its narrow acre it was the law of centuries that here or nowhere must the bones of Israel rest. So the worn and broken tombstones lie piled in close confusion, as though tossed and tumbled by the struggling host beneath.

The Ghetto walls have long been levelled, but the living Jews of Prague still cling to their foetid lanes, though these are being rapidly replaced by fine new streets that promise to eventually transform this quarter into the handsomest part of the town.

At Dresden they advised us not to talk German in Prague. For years racial animosity between the German minority and the Czech majority has raged throughout Bohemia, and to be mistaken for a German in certain streets of Prague is inconvenient to a man whose staying powers in a race are not what once they were. However, we did talk German in certain streets in Prague; it was a case of talking German or nothing. The Czech dialect is said to be of great antiquity and of highly scientific cultivation. Its alphabet contains forty-two letters, suggestive to a stranger of Chinese. It is not a language to be picked up in a hurry. We decided that on the whole there would be less risk to our constitution in keeping to German, and as a matter of fact no harm came to us. The explanation I can only surmise. The Praguer is an exceedingly acute person; some subtle falsity of accent, some slight grammatical inaccuracy, may have crept into our German, revealing to him the fact that, in spite of all appearances to the contrary, we were no true-born Deutscher. I do not assert this; I put it forward as a possibility.

To avoid unnecessary danger, however, we did our sightseeing with the aid of a guide. No guide I have ever come across is perfect. This one had two distinct failings. His English was decidedly weak. Indeed, it was not English at all. I do not know what you would call it. It was not altogether his fault; he had learnt English from a Scotch lady. I understand Scotch fairly well—to keep abreast of modern English literature this is necessary—but to understand broad Scotch talked with a Slavonic accent, occasionally relieved by German modifications, taxes the intelligence. For the first hour it was difficult to rid oneself of the conviction that the man was choking. Every moment we expected him to die on our hands. In the course of the morning we grew accustomed to him, and rid ourselves of the instinct to throw him on his back every time he opened his mouth, and tear his clothes from him. Later, we came to understand a part of what he said, and this led to the discovery of his second failing.

It would seem he had lately invented a hair-restorer, which he had persuaded a local chemist to take up and advertise. Half his time he had been pointing out to us, not the beauties of Prague, but the benefits likely to accrue to the human race from the use of this concoction; and the conventional agreement with which, under the impression he was waxing eloquent concerning views and architecture, we had met his enthusiasm he had attributed to sympathetic interest in this wretched wash of his.

The result was that now there was no keeping him away from the subject. Ruined palaces and crumbling churches he dismissed with curt reference as mere frivolities, encouraging a morbid taste for the decadent. His duty, as he saw it, was not to lead us to dwell upon the ravages of time, but rather to direct our attention to the means of repairing them. What had we to do with broken-headed heroes, or bald-headed saints? Our interest should be surely in the living world; in the maidens with their flowing tresses, or the flowing tresses they might have, by judicious use of 'Kophkeo,' in the young men with their fierce moustaches—as pictured on the label.

Unconsciously, in his own mind, he had divided the world into two sections. The Past ('Before Use'), a sickly disagreeable-looking, uninteresting world. The Future ('After Use') a fat, jolly, God-bless-everybody sort of world; and this unfitted him as a guide to scenes of medieval history.

He sent us each a bottle of the stuff to our hotel. It appeared that in the early part of our converse with him we had, unwittingly, clamoured for it. Personally, I can neither praise it nor condemn it. A long series of disappointments has disheartened me; added to which a permanent atmosphere of paraffin, however faint, is apt to cause remark, especially in the case of a married man. Now, I never try even the sample.

I gave my bottle to George. He asked for it to send to a man he knew in Leeds.   I learnt later that Harris had given him his bottle also, to send to the same man.

A suggestion of onions has clung to this tour since we left Prague.   George has noticed it himself.   He attributes it to the prevalence of garlic in European cooking.

It was in Prague that Harris and I did a kind and friendly thing to George.   We had noticed for some time past that George was getting too fond of Pilsener beer.   This German beer is an insidious drink, especially in hot weather; but it does not do to imbibe too freely of it.   It does not get into your head, but after a time it spoils your waist.   I always say to myself on entering Germany:

'Now, I will drink no German beer.   The white wine of the country, with a little soda-water; perhaps occasionally a glass of Ems or potash.   But beer, never—or, at all events, hardly ever.'

It is a good and useful resolution, which I recommend to all travellers.   I only wish I could keep to it myself.   George, although I urged him, refused to bind himself by any such hard and fast limit.   He said that in moderation German beer was good.

'One glass in the morning,' said George, 'one in the evening, or even two.   That will do no harm to anyone.'

Maybe he was right.   It was his half-dozen glasses that troubled Harris and myself.

'We ought to do something to stop it,' said Harris; 'it is becoming serious.'

'It's hereditary, so he has explained to me,' I answered.   'It seems his family have always been thirsty.'

'There is Apollinaris water,' replied Harris, 'which, I believe, with a little lemon squeezed into it, is practically harmless. What I am thinking about is his figure.   He will lose all his natural elegance.'

We talked the matter over, and, Providence aiding us, we fixed upon a plan.   For the ornamentation of the town a new statue had just been cast.   I forget of whom it was a statue.   I only remember that in the essentials it was the usual sort of street statue, representing the usual sort of gentleman, with the usual stiff neck, riding the usual sort of horse—the horse that always walks on its hind legs, keeping its front paws for beating time. But in detail it possessed individuality.   Instead of the usual sword or baton, the man was holding, stretched out in his hand, his own plumed hat; and the horse, instead of the usual waterfall for a tail, possessed a somewhat attenuated appendage that some-how appeared out of keeping with his ostentatious behaviour. One felt that a horse with a tail like that would not have pranced so much.

It stood in a small square not far from the farther end of the Karlsbrücke, but it stood there only temporarily. Before deciding finally where to fix it, the town authorities had resolved, very sensibly, to judge by practical test where it would look best. Accordingly, they had made three rough copies of the statue—mere wooden profiles, things that would not bear looking at closely, but which, viewed from a little distance, produced all the effect that was necessary. One of these they had set up at the approach to the Franz-Josefsbrücke, a second stood in the open space behind the theatre, and the third in the centre of the Wenzelsplatz.

'If George is not in the secret of this thing,' said Harris—we were walking by ourselves for an hour, he having remained behind in the hotel to write a letter to his aunt—'if he has not observed these statues, then by their aid we will make a better and a thinner man of him, and that this very evening.'

So during dinner we sounded him, judiciously; and finding him ignorant of the matter, we took him out, and led him by side-streets to the place where stood the real statue. George was for looking at it and passing on, as is his way with statues, but we insisted on his pulling up and viewing the thing conscientiously. We walked him round that statue four times, and showed it to him from every possible point of view. I think, on the whole, we rather bored him with the thing, but our object was to impress it upon him. We told him the history of the man who rode upon the horse, the name of the artist who had made the statue, how much it weighed, how much it measured. We worked that statue into his system. By the time we had done with him he knew more about that statue, for the time being, than he knew about anything else. We soaked him in that statue, and only let him go at last on the condition that he would come again with us in the morning, when we could all see it better, and for such purpose we saw to it that he made a note in his pocket-book of the place where the statue stood.

Then we accompanied him to his favourite beer hall, and sat beside him, telling him anecdotes of men who, unaccustomed to German beer, and drinking too much of it, had gone mad and developed homicidal mania; of men who had died young through drinking German beer; of lovers that German beer had been the means of parting for ever from beautiful girls.

At ten o'clock we started to walk back to the hotel. It was a stormy-looking night, with heavy clouds drifting over a light moon. Harris said:

'We won't go back the same way we came, we'll walk back by the river. It is lovely in the moonlight.'

Harris told a sad history, as we walked, about a man he once knew, who is now in a home for harmless imbeciles. He said he recalled the story because it was on just such another night as this that he was walking with that man the very last time he ever saw the poor fellow.' They were strolling down the Thames Embankment, Harris said, and the man frightened him then by persisting that he saw the statue of the Duke of Wellington at the corner of Westminster Bridge, when, as everybody knows, it stands in Piccadilly.

It was at this exact instant that we came in sight of the first of these wooden copies. It occupied the centre of a small, railed-in square a little above us on the opposite side of the way. George suddenly stood still and leant against the wall of the quay.

'What's the matter?' I said. 'Feeling giddy?'

He said: 'I do, a little. Let's rest here a moment.'

He stood there with his eyes glued to the thing. He said, speaking huskily:

'Talking of statues, what always strikes me is how very much one statue is like another statue.'

Harris said: 'I cannot agree with you there—pictures, if you like. Some pictures are very like other pictures, but with a statue there is always something distinctive. Take that statue we saw early in the evening,' continued Harris, 'before we went into the concert hall. It represented a man sitting on a horse. In Prague you will see other statues of men on horses, but nothing at all like that one.'

'Yes they are,' said George; 'they are all alike. It's always the same horse, and it's always the same man. They are all exactly alike. It's idiotic nonsense to say they are not.'

He appeared to be angry with Harris.

'What makes you think so?' I asked.

'What makes me think so?' retorted George, now turning upon me. 'Why, look at that damned thing over there!'

I said: 'What damned thing?'

'Why, that thing,' said George; 'look at it! There is the same

horse with half a tail, standing on its hind legs; the same man
without his hat; the same——'

Harris said: 'You are talking now about the statue we saw in
the Ringplatz.'

'No, I'm not,' replied George; 'I'm talking about the statue
over there.'

'What statue?' said Harris.

George looked at Harris; but Harris is a man who might, with
care, have been a fair amateur actor. His face merely expressed
friendly sorrow, mingled with alarm. Next, George turned his
gaze on me. I endeavoured, so far as lay with me, to copy
Harris's expression, adding to it on my own account a touch of
reproof.

'Will you have a cab?' I said as kindly as I could to George.
'I'll run and get one.'

'What the devil do I want with a cab?' he answered ungra-
ciously. 'Can't you fellows understand a joke? It's like being
out with a couple of confounded old women,' saying which, he
started off across the bridge, leaving us to follow.

'I am so glad that was only a joke of yours,' said Harris, on our
overtaking him. 'I knew a case of softening of the brain that
began——'

'Oh, you're a silly ass!' said George, cutting him short.
'You know everything.'

He was really most unpleasant in his manner.

We took him round by the river side of the theatre. We told
him it was the shortest way, and, as a matter of fact, it was. In
the open space behind the theatre stood the second of these
wooden apparitions. George looked at it, and again stood still.

'What's the matter?' said Harris kindly. 'You are not ill,
are you?'

'I don't believe this is the shortest way,' said George.

'I assure you it is,' persisted Harris.

'Well, I'm going the other,' said George; and he turned and
went: we, as before, following him.

Along the Ferdinand Strasse Harris and I talked about private
lunatic asylums, which, Harris said, were not well managed
in England. He said a friend of his, a patient in a lunatic
asylum——

George said, interrupting: 'You appear to have a large number
of friends in lunatic asylums.'

He said it in a most insulting tone, as though to imply that that is where one would look for the majority of Harris's friends. But Harris did not get angry; he merely replied, quite mildly:

'Well, it really is extraordinary, when one comes to think of it, how many of them have gone that way sooner or later. I get quite nervous sometimes, now.'

At the corner of the Wenzelsplatz, Harris, who was a few steps ahead of us, paused.

'It's a fine street, isn't it?' he said, sticking his hands in his pockets, and gazing up at it admiringly.

George and I followed suit. Two hundred yards away from us, in its very centre, was the third of these ghostly statues. I think it was the best of the three—the most like, the most deceptive. It stood boldly outlined against the wild sky: the horse on its hind legs, with its curiously attenuated tail; the man bare-headed, pointing with his plumed hat to the now entirely visible moon.

'I think, if you don't mind,' said George—he spoke with almost a pathetic ring in his voice, his aggressiveness had completely fallen from him—'that I will have that cab, if there's one handy.'

'I thought you were looking queer,' said Harris kindly. 'It's your head, isn't it?'

'Perhaps it is,' answered George.

'I have noticed it coming on,' said Harris; 'but I didn't like to say anything to you. You fancy you see things, don't you?'

'No, no; it isn't that,' replied George, rather quickly. 'I don't know what it is.'

'I do,' said Harris solemnly, 'and I'll tell you. It's this German beer that you are drinking. I have known a case where a man——'

'Don't tell me about him just now,' said George. 'I dare say it's true, but somehow I don't feel I want to hear about him.'

'You are not used to it,' said Harris.

'I shall give it up from to-night,' said George. 'I think you must be right; it doesn't seem to agree with me.'

We took him home, and saw him to bed. He was very gentle and quite grateful.

One evening later on, after a long day's ride, followed by a most satisfactory dinner, we started him on a big cigar, and, removing things from his reach, told him of this stratagem that for his good we had planned.

'How many copies of that statue did you say we saw?' asked George, after we had finished.

'Three,' replied Harris.

'Only three?' said George. 'Are you sure?'

'Positive,' replied Harris. 'Why?'

'Oh, nothing!' answered George.

But I don't think he quite believed Harris.

From Prague we travelled to Nuremberg, through Carlsbad. Good Germans, when they die, go, they say, to Carlsbad, as good Americans to Paris. This I doubt, seeing that it is a small place with no convenience for a crowd. In Carlsbad, you rise at five, the fashionable hour for promenade, when the band plays under the Colonnade, and the Sprudel is filled with a packed throng over a mile long, being from six to eight in the morning. Here you may hear more languages spoken than the Tower of Babel could have echoed. Polish Jews and Russian princes, Chinese mandarins and Turkish pashas, Norwegians looking as if they had stepped out of Ibsen's plays, women from the Boulevardes, Spanish grandees and English countesses, mountaineers from Montenegro and millionaires from Chicago, you will find every dozen yards. Every luxury in the world Carlsbad provides for its visitors, with the one exception of pepper. That you cannot get within five miles of the town for money; what you can get there for love is not worth taking away. Pepper, to the liver brigade that forms four-fifths of Carlsbad's customers, is poison; and, prevention being better than cure, it is carefully kept out of the neighbourhood. 'Pepper parties' are formed in Carlsbad to journey to some place without the boundary, and there indulge in pepper orgies.

Nuremberg, if one expects a town of medieval appearance, disappoints. Quaint corners, picturesque glimpses, there are in plenty, but everywhere they are surrounded and intruded upon by the modern, and even what is ancient is not nearly so ancient as one thought it was. After all, a town, like a woman, is only as old as it looks; and Nuremberg is still a comfortable-looking dame, its age somewhat difficult to conceive under its fresh paint and stucco in the blaze of the gas and electric light. Still, looking closely, you may see its wrinkled walls and grey towers.

CHAPTER IX

*Harris breaks the law—The helpful man: The dangers that beset him—
George sets forth upon a career of crime—Those to whom Germany
would come as a boon and a blessing—The English Sinner: His dis-
appointments—The German Sinner: His exceptional advantages—
What you may not do with your bed—An inexpensive vice—The
German dog: His simple goodness—The misbehaviour of the beetle—
A people that go the way they ought to go—The German small boy:
His love of legality—How to go astray with a perambulator—The
German student: His chastened wilfulness.*

ALL three of us, by some means or another, managed, between
Nuremberg and the Black Forest, to get into trouble.

Harris led off at Stuttgart by insulting an official.   Stuttgart is
a charming town, clean and bright, a smaller Dresden.   It has
the additional attraction of containing little that one need to go
out of one's way to see: a medium-sized picture gallery, a small
museum of antiquities, and half a palace, and you are through
with the entire thing and can enjoy yourself.   Harris did not
know it was an official he was insulting.   He took it for a fireman
(it looked like a fireman), and he called it a 'dummer Esel.'

In Germany you are not permitted to call an official a 'silly
ass,' but undoubtedly this particular man was one.   What had
happened was this: Harris in the Stadgarten, anxious to get out,
and seeing a gate open before him, had stepped over a wire into
the street.   Harris maintains he never saw it, but undoubtedly
there was hanging to the wire a notice 'Durchgang Verboten!'
The man, who was standing near the gate, stopped Harris, and
pointed out to him this notice.   Harris thanked him, and passed
on.   The man came after him, and explained that treatment of
the matter in such offhand way could not be allowed; what was
necessary to put the business right was that Harris should step
back over the wire into the garden.   Harris pointed out to the
man that the notice said 'going through forbidden,' and that,
therefore, by re-entering the garden that way he would be
infringing the law a second time.   The man saw this for himself,
and suggested that to get over the difficulty Harris should go back
into the garden by the proper entrance, which was round the
corner, and afterwards immediately come out again by the same

101

gate.   Then it was that Harris called the man a silly ass.   That delayed us a day, and cost Harris forty marks.

I followed suit at Carlsruhe, by stealing a bicycle.   I did not mean to steal the bicycle; I was merely trying to be useful.   The train was on the point of starting when I noticed, as I thought, Harris's bicycle still in the goods van.   No one was about to help me.   I jumped into the van and hauled it out, only just in time. Wheeling it down the platform in triumph, I came across Harris's bicycle, standing against a wall behind some milk-cans.   The bicycle I had secured was not Harris's, but some other man's.

It was an awkward situation.   In England, I should have gone to the station-master and explained my mistake.   But in Germany they are not content with your explaining a little matter of this sort to one man: they take you round and get you to explain it to about half a dozen; and if any one of the half-dozen happens not to be handy, or not to have time just then to listen to you, they have a habit of leaving you over for the night to finish your explanation the next morning.   I thought I would just put the thing out of sight, and then, without making any fuss or show, take a short walk.   I found a woodshed, which seemed just the very place, and was wheeling the bicycle into it when, unfortunately, a red-hatted railway official, with the airs of a retired field-marshal, caught sight of me and came up.   He said:

'What are you doing with that bicycle?'

I said: 'I am going to put it in this woodshed out of the way.' I tried to convey by my tone that I was performing a kind and thoughtful action, for which the railway officials ought to thank me; but he was unresponsive.

'Is it your bicycle?' he said.

'Well, not exactly,' I replied.

'Whose is it?' he asked quite sharply.

'I can't tell you,' I answered.   'I don't know whose bicycle it is.'

'Where did you get it from?' was his next question.   There was a suspiciousness about his tone that was almost insulting.

'I got it,' I answered, with as much calm dignity as at the moment I could assume, 'out of the train.   The fact is,' I continued frankly, 'I have made a mistake.'

He did not allow me time to finish.   He merely said he thought so, too, and blew a whistle.

Recollection of the subsequent proceedings is not, so far as I am concerned, amusing.   By a miracle of good luck—they say providence watches over certain of us—the incident happened in Carlsruhe, where I possess a German friend, an official of some importance. Upon what would have been my fate had the station not been at Carlsruhe, or had my friend been from home, I do not care to dwell; as it was I got off, as the saying is, by the skin of my teeth. I should like to add that I left Carlsruhe without a stain upon my character, but that would not be the truth. My going scot free is regarded in police circles there to this day as a grave miscarriage of justice.

But all lesser sin sinks into insignificance beside the lawlessness of George. The bicycle incident had thrown us all into confusion, with the result that we lost George altogether. It transpired subsequently that he was waiting for us outside the police court; but this at the time we did not know. We thought, maybe, he had gone on to Baden by himself; and anxious to get away from Carlsruhe, and not, perhaps, thinking out things too clearly, we jumped into the next train that came up and proceeded thither. When George, tired of waiting, returned to the station, he found us gone and he found his luggage gone. Harris had his ticket; I was acting as banker to the party, so that he had in his pocket only some small change. Excusing himself upon these grounds, he thereupon commenced deliberately a career of crime that, reading it later, as set forth baldly in the official summons, made the hair of Harris and myself almost to stand on end.

German travelling, it may be explained, is somewhat complicated. You buy a ticket at the station you start from for the place you want to go to. You might think this would enable you to get there, but it does not. When your train comes up, you attempt to swarm into it; but the guard magnificently waves you away. Where are your credentials? You show him your ticket. He explains to you that by itself that is of no service whatever; you have only taken the first step towards travelling; you must go back to the booking-office and get in addition what is called a '*schnellzug* ticket.' With this you return, thinking your troubles over. You are allowed to get in, so far so good. But you must not sit down anywhere, and you must not stand still, and you must not wander about. You must take another ticket, this time what is called a '*platz* ticket,' which entitles you to a place for a certain distance.

What a man could do who persisted in taking nothing but the one ticket, I have often wondered. Would he be entitled to run behind the train on the six-foot way? Or could he stick a label on himself and get into the goods van? Again, what could be done with the man who, having taken his *schnellzug* ticket, obstinately refused, or had not the money to take a *platz* ticket: would they let him lie in the umbrella rack, or allow him to hang himself out of the window?

To return to George, he had just sufficient money to take a third-class slow train ticket to Baden, and that was all. To avoid the inquisitiveness of the guard, he waited till the train was moving, and then jumped in.

That was his first sin:
> (*a*) Entering a train in motion;
> (*b*) After being warned not to do so by an official.

Second sin:
> (*a*) Travelling in train of superior class to that for which ticket was held.
> (*b*) Refusing to pay difference when demanded by an official (George says he did not 'refuse'; he simply told the man he had not got it.)

Third sin:
> (*a*) Travelling in carriage of superior class to that for which ticket was held.
> (*b*) Refusing to pay difference when demanded by an official. (Again George disputes the accuracy of the report. He turned his pockets out, and offered the man all he had, which was about eightpence in German money. He offered to go into a third class, but there was no third class. He offered to go into the goods van, but they would not hear of it.)

Fourth sin:
> (*a*) Occupying seat, and not paying for same.
> (*b*) Loitering about corridor. (As they would not let him sit down without paying, and as he could not pay, it was difficult to see what else he could do.)

But explanations are held as no excuse in Germany; and his journey from Carlsruhe to Baden was one of the most expensive perhaps on record.

Reflecting upon the ease and frequency with which one gets into trouble here in Germany, one is led to the conclusion that this country would come as a boon and a blessing to the average

young Englishman. To the medical student, to the eater of
dinners at the Temple, to the subaltern on leave, life in London
is a wearisome proceeding. The healthy Briton takes his
pleasure lawlessly, or it is no pleasure to him. Nothing that he
may do affords to him any genuine satisfaction. To be in trouble
of some sort is his only idea of bliss. Now, England affords him
small opportunity in this respect; to get himself into a scrape
requires a good deal of persistence on the part of the young
Englishman.

I spoke on this subject one day with our senior churchwarden.
It was the morning of the 10th of November, and we were both
of us glancing, somewhat anxiously, through the police reports.
The usual batch of young men had been summoned for creating
the usual disturbance the night before at the Criterion. My
friend the churchwarden has boys of his own, and a nephew of
mine, upon whom I am keeping a fatherly eye, is by a fond
mother supposed to be in London for the sole purpose of
studying engineering. No names we knew happened, by fortunate chance, to be in the list of those detained in custody, and,
relieved, we fell to moralizing upon the folly and depravity of
youth.

'It is very remarkable,' said my friend the churchwarden,
'how the Criterion retains its position in this respect. It was just
so when I was young; the evening always wound up with a row at
the Criterion.'

'So meaningless,' I remarked.

'So monotonous,' he replied. 'You have no idea,' he continued, a dreamy expression stealing over his furrowed face, 'how
unutterably tired one can become of the walk from Piccadilly
Circus to the Vine Street Police Court. Yet, what else was there
for us to do? Simply nothing. Sometimes we would put out a
street lamp, and a man would come round and light it again. If
one insulted a policeman, he simply took no notice. He did not
even know he was being insulted; or, if he did, he seemed not to
care. You could fight a Covent Garden porter, if you fancied
yourself at that sort of thing. Generally speaking, the porter got
the best of it; and when he did it cost you five shillings, and when
he did not the price was half a sovereign. I could never see
much excitement in that particular sport. I tried driving a
hansom cab once. That has always been regarded as the acme of
modern Tom and Jerryism. I stole it late one night from outside a public-house in Dean Street, and the first thing that

happened to me was that I was hailed in Golden Square by an old lady surrounded by three children, two of them crying and the third one half asleep.   Before I could get away she had shot the brats into the cab, taken my number, paid me, so she said, a shilling over the legal fare, and directed me to an address a little beyond what she called North Kensington.   As a matter of fact, the place turned out to be the other side of Willesden.   The horse was tired, and the journey took us well over two hours.   It was the slowest lark I ever remember being concerned in.   I tried once or twice to persuade the children to let me take them back to the old lady: but every time I opened the trap-door to speak to them the youngest one, a boy, started screaming; and when I offered other drivers to transfer the job to them most of them replied in the words of a song, popular about that period: "Oh, George, don't you think you're going just a bit too far?" One man offered to take home to my wife any last message I might be thinking of, whilst another promised to organize a party to come and dig me out in the spring.   When I mounted the dickey I had imagined myself driving a peppery old colonel to some lonesome and cabless region, half a dozen miles from where he wanted to go, and there leaving him upon the kerbstone to swear.   About that there might have been good sport or there might not, according to circumstances and the colonel.   The idea of a trip to an outlying suburb in charge of a nursery full of helpless infants had never occurred to me.   No, London,' concluded my friend the churchwarden with a sigh, 'affords but limited opportunity to the lover of the illegal.'

Now, in Germany, on the other hand, trouble is to be had for the asking.   There are many things in Germany that you must not do that are quite easy to do.   To any young Englishman yearning to get himself into a scrape, and finding himself hampered in his own country, I would advise a single ticket to Germany; a return, lasting as it does only a month, might prove a waste.

In the Police Guide of the Fatherland he will find set forth a list of the things the doing of which will bring to him interest and excitement.   In Germany you must not hang your bed out of the window.   He might begin with that.   By waving his bed out of the window he could get into trouble before he had his breakfast.   At home he might hang himself out of a window, and nobody would mind much, provided he did not obstruct anybody's ancient lights or break away and injure any passer underneath.

In Germany you must not wear fancy dress in the streets. A Highlander of my acquaintance who came to pass the winter in Dresden spent the first few days of his residence there in arguing this question with the Saxon Government. They asked him what he was doing in those clothes. He was not an amiable man. He answered, he was wearing them. They asked him why he was wearing them. He replied to keep himself warm. They told him frankly that they did not believe him, and sent him back to his lodgings in a closed landau. The personal testimony of the English minister was necessary to assure the authorities that the Highland garb was the customary dress of many respectable, law-abiding British subjects. They accepted the statement, as diplomatically bound, but retain their private opinion to this day. The English tourist they have grown accustomed to; but a Leicestershire gentleman, invited to hunt with some German officers, on appearing outside his hotel, was promptly marched off, horse and all, to explain his frivolity at the police court.

Another thing you must not do in the streets of German towns is to feed horses, mules, or donkeys, whether your own or those belonging to other people. If a passion seizes you to feed somebody else's horse, you must make an appointment with the animal, and the meal must take place in some properly authorized place. You must not break glass or china in the street, nor, in fact, in any public resort whatever; and if you do, you must pick up all the pieces. What you are to do with the pieces when you have gathered them together I cannot say. The only thing I know for certain is that you are not permitted to throw them anywhere, to leave them anywhere, or apparently to part with them in any way whatever. Presumably, you are expected to carry them about with you until you die, and then be buried with them; or, maybe, you are allowed to swallow them.

In German streets you must not shoot with a crossbow. The German law-maker does not content himself with the misdeeds of the average man—the crime one feels one wants to do, but must not: he worries himself imagining all the things a wandering maniac might do. In Germany there is no law against a man standing on his head in the middle of the road; the idea has not occurred to them. One of these days a German statesman, visiting a circus and seeing acrobats, will reflect upon this omission. Then he will straightway set to work and frame a clause forbidding people from standing on their heads in the

middle of the road, and fixing a fine. This is the charm of
German law: misdemeanour in Germany has its fixed price.
You are not kept awake all night, as in England, wondering
whether you will get off with a caution, be fined forty shillings,
or, catching the magistrate in an unhappy moment for yourself,
get seven days. You know exactly what your fun is going to
cost you. You can spread out your money on the table, open
your Police Guide, and plan out your holiday to a fifty pfennig
piece. For a really cheap evening, I would recommend walking
on the wrong side of the pavement after being cautioned not

You must not shoot with a crossbow

to do so. I calculate that by choosing your district and keeping
to the quiet side-streets you could walk for a whole evening on
the wrong side of the pavement at a cost of little over three
marks.

In German towns you must not ramble about after dark 'in
droves.' I am not quite sure how many constitute a 'drove,'
and no official to whom I have spoken on this subject has felt
himself competent to fix the exact number. I once put it to a
German friend who was starting for the theatre with his wife,
his mother-in-law, five children of his own, his sister and her
fiancé, and two nieces, if he did not think he was running a risk
under this by-law. He did not take my suggestion as a joke.
He cast an eye over the group.

'Oh, I don't think so,' he said; 'you see, we are all one family.'

'The paragraph says nothing about its being a family drove
or not,' I replied; 'it simply says "drove." I do not mean it in

any uncomplimentary sense, but, speaking etymologically, I am inclined personally to regard your collection as a "drove." Whether the police will take the same view or not remains to be seen. I am merely warning you.'

My friend himself was inclined to pooh-pooh my fears; but his wife thinking it better not to run any risk of having the party broken up by the police at the very beginning of the evening, they divided, arranging to come together again in the theatre lobby.

Another passion you must restrain in Germany is that prompting you to throw things out of window. Cats are no excuse. During the first week of my residence in Germany I was awakened incessantly by cats. One night I got mad. I collected a small arsenal—two or three pieces of coal, a few hard pears, a couple of candle ends, an odd egg I found on the kitchen table, an empty soda-water bottle, and a few articles of that sort—and, opening the window, bombarded the spot from where the noise appeared to come. I do not suppose I hit anything; I never knew a man who did hit a cat, even when he could see it, except, maybe, by accident when aiming at something else. I have known crack shots, winners of Queen's prizes—those sort of men—shoot with shot-guns at cats fifty yards away, and never hit a hair. I have often thought that, instead of bull's-eyes, running deer, and that rubbish, the really superior marksman would be he who could boast that he had shot the cat.

But, anyhow, they moved off; maybe the egg annoyed them. I had noticed when I picked it up that it did not look a good egg; and I went back to bed again, thinking the incident closed. Ten minutes afterwards there came a violent ringing of the electric bell. I tried to ignore it, but it was too persistent, and, putting on my dressing-gown, I went down to the gate. A policeman was standing there. He had all the things I had been throwing out of the window in a little heap in front of him, all except the egg. He had evidently been collecting them. He said:

'Are these things yours?'

I said: 'They were mine, but personally I have done with them. Anybody can have them—you can have them.'

He ignored my offer. He said:

'You threw these things out of window.'

'You are right,' I admitted; 'I did.'

'Why did you throw them out of window?' he asked. A German policeman has his code of questions arranged for him; he never varies them, and he never omits one.

'I threw them out of the window at some cats,' I answered.

'What cats?' he asked.

It was the sort of question a German policeman would ask. I replied with as much sarcasm as I could put into my accent that I was ashamed to say I could not tell him what cats. I explained that, personally, they were strangers to me; but I offered, if the police would call all the cats in the district together, to come round and see if I could recognize them by their yawl.

The German policeman does not understand a joke, which is perhaps on the whole just as well, for I believe there is a heavy fine for joking with any German uniform; they call it 'treating an official with contumely.' He merely replied that it was not the duty of the police to help me recognize the cats; their duty was merely to fine me for throwing things out of window.

I asked what a man was supposed to do in Germany when woke up night after night by cats, and he explained that I could lodge an information against the owner of the cat, when the police would proceed to caution him, and, if necessary, order the cat to be destroyed. Who was going to destroy the cat, and what the cat would be doing during the process, he did not explain.

I asked him how he proposed I should discover the owner of the cat. He thought for a while, and then suggested that I might follow it home. I did not feel inclined to argue with him any more after that; I should only have said things that would have made the matter worse. As it was, that night's sport cost me twelve marks; and not a single one of the four German officials who interviewed me on the subject could see anything ridiculous in the proceedings from beginning to end.

But in Germany most human faults and follies sink into comparative insignificance beside the enormity of walking on the grass. Nowhere, and under no circumstances, may you at any time in Germany walk on the grass. Grass in Germany is quite a fetish. To put your foot on German grass would be as great a sacrilege as to dance a hornpipe on a Mohammedan's praying-mat. The very dogs respect German grass; no German dog would dream of putting a paw on it. If you see a dog scampering across the grass in Germany, you may know for certain that it is the dog of some unholy foreigner. In England, when we want to keep dogs out of places, we put up wire netting, six feet high

supported by buttresses, and defended on the top by spikes.   In
Germany, they put a notice-board in the middle of the place,
'Hunden verboten,' and a dog that has German blood in its veins
looks at that notice-board and walks away.   In a German park
I have seen a gardener step gingerly with felt boots on to a grass-
plot, and removing therefrom a beetle, place it gravely but firmly

The beetle and the gardener

on the gravel; which done, he stood sternly watching the beetle,
to see that it did not try to get back on the grass; and the beetle,
looking utterly ashamed of itself, walked hurriedly down the
gutter, and turned up the path marked 'Ausgang.'

In German parks separate roads are devoted to the different
orders of the community, and no one person, at peril of liberty
and fortune, may go upon another person's road.   There are
special paths for 'wheel-riders' and special paths for 'foot-goers,'
avenues for 'horse-riders,' roads for people in light vehicles, and

roads for people in heavy vehicles; ways for children and for 'alone ladies.' That no particular route has yet been set aside for bald-headed men or 'new women' has always struck me as an omission.

In the Grosse Garten in Dresden I once came across an old lady, standing, helpless and bewildered, in the centre of seven tracks. Each was guarded by a threatening notice, warning everybody off it but the person for whom it was intended.

'I am sorry to trouble you,' said the old lady, on learning I could speak English and read German, 'but would you mind telling me what I am and where I have to go?'

I inspected her carefully. I came to the conclusion that she was a 'grown-up' and a 'foot-goer,' and pointed out her path. She looked at it, and seemed disappointed.

'But I don't want to go down there,' she said; 'mayn't I go this way?'

'Great heavens, no, madam!' I replied. 'That path is reserved for children.'

'But I wouldn't do them any harm,' said the old lady, with a smile. She did not look the sort of old lady who would have done them any harm.

'Madam,' I replied, 'if it rested with me, I would trust you down that path, though my own first-born were at the other end; but I can only inform you of the laws of this country. For you, a full-grown woman, to venture down that path is to go to certain fine, if not imprisonment. There is your path, marked plainly— "Nur für Fussgänger," and if you will follow my advice, you will hasten down it; you are not allowed to stand here and hesitate.'

'It doesn't lead a bit in the direction I want to go,' said the old lady.

'It leads in the direction you *ought* to want to go,' I replied, and we parted.

In the German parks there are special seats labelled, 'Only for grown-ups' ('Nur für Erwachsene'), and the German small boy, anxious to sit down and reading that notice, passes by, and hunts for a seat on which children are permitted to rest; and there he seats himself, careful not to touch the woodwork with his muddy boots. Imagine a seat in Regent's or St James's Park labelled 'Only for grown-ups'! Every child for five miles round would be trying to get on that seat, and hauling other children off who were on. As for any 'grown-up,' he would never be able to get within half a mile of that seat for the crowd. The German small boy, who has accidentally sat down on such without noticing, rises with a start when his error is pointed out to him, and goes away with downcast head, blushing to the roots of his hair with shame and regret.

Not that the German child is neglected by a paternal Government. In German parks and public gardens special places (*Spielplätze*) are provided for him, each one supplied with a heap of sand. There he can play to his heart's content at making mud pies and building sand castles. To the German child a pie made of any other mud than this would appear an immoral pie. It would give to him no satisfaction: his soul would revolt against it.

The German boy

'That pie,' he would say to himself, 'was not, as it should have been, made of Government mud specially set apart for the purpose; it was not manufactured in the place planned and maintained by the Government for the making of mud pies. It can bring no real blessing with it; it is a lawless pie.' And until his father had paid the proper fine, and he had received his proper licking, his conscience would continue to trouble him.

Another excellent piece of material for obtaining excitement in Germany is the simple domestic perambulator. What you may do with a *kinderwagen*, as it is called, and what you may not, covers pages of German law; after the reading of which, you conclude that the man who can push a perambulator through a German town without breaking the law was meant for a diplomatist. You must not loiter with a perambulator, and you must not go too fast. You must not get in anybody's way with a perambulator, and if anybody gets in your way you must get out of their way. If you want to stop with a perambulator, you must go to a place specially appointed where perambulators may stop; and when you get there you *must* stop. You must not cross the road with a perambulator; if you and the baby happen to live on the other side, that is your fault. You must not leave your

perambulator anywhere, and only in certain places can you take
it with you.   I should say that in Germany you could go out
with a perambulator and get into enough trouble in half an hour
to last you for a month.   Any young Englishman anxious for a
row with the police could not do better than come over to Germany and bring his perambulator with him.

In Germany you must not leave your front door unlocked after
ten o'clock at night, and you must not play the piano in your own
house after eleven.   In England I have never felt I wanted to
play the piano myself, or to hear anyone else play it, after eleven
o'clock at night; but that is a very different thing to being told
that you must not play it.   Here, in Germany, I never feel that I
really care for the piano until eleven o'clock, then I could sit and
listen to the 'Maiden's Prayer,' or the Overture to 'Zampa,' with
pleasure.   To the law-loving German, on the other hand, music
after eleven o'clock at night ceases to be music: it becomes sin,
and as such gives him no satisfaction.

The only individual throughout Germany who ever dreams of
taking liberties with the law is the German student, and he only
to a certain well-defined point.   By custom, certain privileges
are permitted to him, but even these are strictly limited and
clearly understood.   For instance, the German student may get
drunk and fall asleep in the gutter with no other penalty than
that of having the next morning to tip the policeman who has
found him and brought him home.   But for this purpose he
must choose the gutters of side-streets.   The German student,
conscious of the rapid approach of oblivion, uses all his remaining
energy to get round the corner where he may collapse without
anxiety.   In certain districts he may ring bells.   The rent of
flats in these localities is lower than in other quarters of the
town; while the difficulty is further met by each family preparing
for itself a secret code of bell-ringing, by means of which it is
known whether the summons is genuine or not.   When visiting
such a household late at night it is well to be acquainted with this
code, or you may, if persistent, get a bucket of water thrown
over you.

Also the German student is allowed to put out lights at night,
but there is a prejudice against his putting out too many.   The
larky German student generally keeps count, contenting himself
with half a dozen lights per night.   Likewise, he may shout and
sing as he walks home up till half past two; and at certain
restaurants it is permitted to him to put his arm round the

fraulein's waist.   To prevent any suggestion of unseemliness,
the waitresses at restaurants frequented by students are always
carefully selected from among a staid and elderly class of women,
by reason of which the German student can enjoy the delights of
flirtation without fear and without reproach to anyone.

They are a law-abiding people, the Germans.

CHAPTER X

FROM Baden, about which it need only be said that it is a pleasure
resort singularly like other pleasure resorts of the same description, we started bicycling in earnest. We planned a ten-days'
tour, which, while completing the Black Forest, should include
a spin down the Donau-Thal, which for the twenty miles from
Tuttlingen to Sigmaringen is, perhaps, the finest valley in Germany; the Danube stream here winding its narrow way past old-
world unspoilt villages; past ancient monasteries, nestling in
green pastures, where still the bare-footed and bare-headed friar,
his rope girdle tight about his loins, shepherds, with crook in
hand, his sheep upon the hill sides; through rocky woods;
between sheer walls of cliff, whose every towering crag stands
crowned with ruined fortress, church, or castle; together with a
blick at the Vosges mountains, where half the population is
bitterly pained if you speak to them in French, the other half
being insulted when you address them in German, and the whole
indignantly contemptuous at the first sound of English; a state
of things that renders conversation with the stranger somewhat
nervous work.

We did not succeed in carrying out our programme in its
entirety, for the reason that human performance lags ever
behind human intention. It is easy to say and believe at three
o'clock in the afternoon that: 'We will rise at five, breakfast
lightly at half past, and start away at six.'

'Then we shall be well on our way before the heat of the day
sets in,' remarks one.

'This time of the year, the early morning is really the best part
of the day. Don't you think so?' adds another.

'Oh, undoubtedly.'

'So cool and fresh.'

'And the half-lights are so exquisite.'

The first morning one maintains one's vows. The party assembles at half past five. It is very silent; individually, somewhat snappy; inclined to grumble with its food, also with most other things; the atmosphere charged with compressed irritability seeking its vent. In the evening the Tempter's voice is heard:

'I think if we got off by half past six, sharp, that would be time enough?'

The voice of Virtue protests, faintly: 'It will be breaking our resolution.'

The Tempter replies: 'Resolutions were made for man, not man for resolutions.' The devil can paraphrase Scripture for his own purpose. 'Besides, it is disturbing the whole hotel; think of the poor servants.'

The voice of Virtue continues, but even feebler: 'But everybody gets up early in these parts.'

'They would not if they were not obliged to, poor things! Say breakfast at half past six, punctual; that will be disturbing nobody.'

Thus Sin masquerades under the guise of Good, and one sleeps till six, explaining to one's conscience, who, however, doesn't believe it, that one does this because of unselfish consideration for others. I have known such consideration extend until seven of the clock.

Likewise, distance measured with a pair of compasses is not precisely the same as when measured by the leg.

'Ten miles an hour for seven hours: seventy miles. A nice easy day's work.'

'There are some stiff hills to climb?'

'The other side to come down. Say, eight miles an hour, and call it sixty miles. *Gott in Himmel!* if we can't average eight miles an hour, we had better go in bath-chairs.' It does seem somewhat impossible to do less, on paper.

But at four o'clock in the afternoon the voice of Duty rings less trumpet-toned:

'Well, I suppose we ought to be getting on.'

'Oh, there's no hurry! don't fuss. Lovely view from here, isn't it?'

'Very. Don't forget we are twenty-five miles from St Blasien.'

'How far?'

'Twenty-five miles, a little over if anything.'

'Do you mean to say we have only come thirty-five miles?'

'That's all.'

'Nonsense. I don't believe that map of yours.'

'It is impossible, you know. We have been riding steadily ever since the first thing this morning.'

'No, we haven't. We didn't get away till eight, to begin with.'

'Quarter to eight.'

'Well, quarter to eight; and every half-dozen miles we have stopped.'

'We have only stopped to look at the view. It's no good coming to see a country and then not seeing it.'

'And we have had to pull up some stiff hills.'

'Besides, it has been an exceptionally hot day to-day.'

'Well, don't forget St Blasien is twenty-five miles off, that's all.'

'Any more hills?'

'Yes, two; up and down.'

'I thought you said it was downhill into St Blasien?'

'So it is for the last ten miles. We are twenty-five miles from St Blasien here.'

'Isn't there anywhere between here and St Blasien? What's that little place there on the lake?'

'It isn't St Blasien, or anywhere near it. There's a danger in beginning that sort of thing.'

'There's a danger in overworking oneself. One should study moderation in all things. Pretty little place, that Titisee, according to the map; looks as if there would be good air there.'

'All right, I'm agreeable. It was you fellows who suggested our making for St Blasien.'

'Oh, I'm not so keen on St Blasien! poky little place, down in a valley. This Titisee, I should say, was ever so much nicer.'

'Quite near, isn't it?'

'Five miles.'

General chorus: 'We'll stop at Titisee.'

George made discovery of this difference between theory and practice on the very first day of our ride.

'I thought,' said George—he was riding the single, Harris and I being a little ahead on the tandem—'that the idea was to train up the hills and ride down them.'

'So it is,' answered Harris, 'as a general rule. But the trains don't go up *every* hill in the Black Forest.'

'Somehow, I felt a suspicion that they wouldn't,' growled George; and for a while silence reigned.

'Besides,' remarked Harris, who had evidently been ruminating the subject, 'you would not wish to have nothing but downhill, surely. It would not be playing the game. One must take a little rough with one's smooth.'

Again there returned silence, broken after a while by George this time.

'Don't you two fellows over-exert yourselves merely on my account,' said George.

'How do you mean?' asked Harris.

'I mean,' answered George, 'that where a train does happen to be going up these hills, don't you put aside the idea of taking it for fear of outraging my finer feelings. Personally, I am prepared to go up all these hills in a railway train, even if it's not playing the game. I'll square the thing with my conscience; I've been up at seven every day for a week now, and I calculate it owes me a bit. Don't you consider me in the matter at all.'

We promised to bear this in mind, and again the ride continued in dogged dumbness, until it was again broken by George.

'What bicycle did you say this was of yours?' asked George.

Harris told him. I forget of what particular manufacture it happened to be; it is immaterial.

'Are you sure?' persisted George.

'Of course I am sure,' answered Harris. 'Why, what's the matter with it?'

'Well, it doesn't come up to the poster,' said George, 'that's all.'

'What poster?' asked Harris.

'The poster advertising this particular brand of cycle,' explained George. 'I was looking at one on a hoarding in Sloane Street only a day or two before we started. A man was riding this make of machine, a man with a banner in his hand: he wasn't doing any work, that was clear as daylight; he was just sitting on the thing and drinking in the air. The cycle was going of its own accord, and going well. This thing of yours leaves all the work to me. It is a lazy brute of a machine; if you don't shove, it simply does nothing. I should complain about it, if I were you.'

When one comes to think of it, few bicycles do realize the poster. On only one poster that I can recollect have I seen the rider represented as doing any work. But then this man was being pursued by a bull. In ordinary cases the object of the artist is to convince the hesitating neophyte that the sport of bicycling consists in sitting on a luxurious saddle, and being moved rapidly in the direction you wish to go by unseen heavenly powers.

Generally speaking, the rider is a lady, and then one feels that, for perfect bodily rest combined with entire freedom from mental anxiety, slumber upon a water-bed cannot compare with bicycle-riding upon a hilly road. No fairy travelling on a summer cloud could take things more easily than does the bicycle girl, according to the poster. Her costume for cycling in hot weather is ideal. Old-fashioned landladies might refuse her lunch, it is true; and a narrow-minded police force might desire to secure her, and wrap her in a rug preliminary to summoning her. But such she heeds not. Uphill and downhill, through traffic that might tax the ingenuity of a cat, over road surfaces, calculated to break the average steam-roller she passes, a vision of idle loveliness; her fair hair streaming to the wind, her sylph-like form poised airily, one foot upon the saddle, the other resting lightly upon the lamp. Sometimes she condescends to sit down on the saddle; then she puts her feet on the rests, lights a cigarette, and waves above her head a Chinese lantern.

Less often, it is a mere male thing that rides the machine. He is not so accomplished an acrobat as is the lady; but simple tricks such as standing on the saddle and waving flags, drinking beer or beef-tea while riding, he can and does perform. Something, one supposes, he must do to occupy his mind: sitting still hour after hour on this machine, having no work to do, nothing to think about, must pall upon any man of active temperament. Thus it is that we see him riding on his pedals as he nears the top of some high hill to apostrophize the sun, or address poetry to the surrounding scenery.

Occasionally the poster pictures a pair of cyclists; and then one grasps the fact how much superior for purposes of flirtation is the modern bicycle to the old-fashioned parlour or the played-out garden gate. He and she mount their bicycles, being careful, of course, that such are of the right make. After that they have nothing to think about but the old sweet tale. Down shady lanes, through busy towns on market days, merrily roll the wheels of the 'Bermondsey Company's Bottom Bracket Britain's Best,' or of the 'Camberwell Company's Jointless Eureka.'

They need no pedalling; they require no guiding. Give them their heads, and tell them what time you want to get home, and that is all they ask. While Edwin leans from his saddle to whisper the dear old nothings in Angelina's ear, while Angelina's face, to hide its blushes, is turned towards the horizon at the back, the magic bicycles pursue their even course.

And the sun is always shining, and the roads are always dry. No stern parent rides behind, no interfering aunt beside, no demon small boy brother is peeping round the corner, there never comes a skid. Ah me! Why were there no 'Britain's Best' nor 'Camberwell Eurekas' to be hired when *we* were young?

Or maybe the 'Britain's Best' or the 'Camberwell Eureka' stands leaning against a gate; maybe it is tired. It has worked hard all the afternoon, carrying these young people. Mercifully minded they have dismounted, to give the machine a rest. They sit upon the grass beneath the shade of graceful boughs; it is long and dry grass. A stream flows by their feet. All is rest and peace.

That is ever the idea the cycle poster artist sets himself to convey—rest and peace.

But I am wrong in saying that no cyclist, according to the poster, ever works. Now I come to reflect, I have seen posters representing gentlemen on cycles working very hard—over-working themselves, one might almost say. They are thin and haggard with the toil, the perspiration stands upon their brow in beads; you feel that if there is another hill beyond the poster they must either get off or die. But this is the result of their own folly. This happens because they will persist in riding a machine of an inferior make. Were they riding a 'Putney Popular' or 'Battersea Bounder,' such as the sensible young man in the centre of the poster rides, then all this unnecessary labour would be saved to them. Then all required of them would be, as in gratitude bound, to look happy; perhaps, occasionally to back-pedal a little when the machine in its youthful buoyancy loses its head for a moment and dashes on too swiftly.

You tired young men, sitting dejectedly on milestones, too spent to heed the steady rain that soaks you through; you weary maidens, with the straight, damp hair, anxious about the time, longing to swear, not knowing how; you stout bald men, vanishing visibly as you pant and grunt along the endless road; you purple, dejected matrons, plying with pain the slow,

unwilling wheel; why did you not see to it that you bought a
'Britain's Best' or a 'Camberwell Eureka'? Why are these
bicycles of inferior make so prevalent throughout the land?

Or is it with bicycling as with all other things: does Life at no
point realize the Poster?

The one thing in Germany that never fails to charm and
fascinate me is the German dog. In England one grows tired of
the old breeds, one knows them all so well: the mastiff, the plum-
pudding dog, the terrier (black, white, or rough-haired, as the
case may be, but always quarrelsome), the collie, the bulldog;
never anything new. Now in Germany you get variety. You
come across dogs the like of which you have never seen before:
that until you hear them bark you do not know are dogs. It is all
so fresh, so interesting. George stopped a dog in Sigmaringen
and drew our attention to it. It suggested a cross between a
codfish and a poodle. I would not like to be positive it was *not*
a cross between a codfish and a poodle. Harris tried to photograph it, but it ran up a fence and disappeared through some
bushes.

I do not know what the German breeder's idea is; at present he
retains his secret. George suggests he is aiming at a griffin.
There is much to bear out this theory, and, indeed, in one or two
cases I have come across success on these lines would seem to
have been almost achieved. Yet I cannot bring myself to
believe that such are anything more than mere accidents. The
German is practical, and I fail to see the object of a griffin. If
mere quaintness of design be desired, is there not already the
Dachshund! What more is needed? Besides, about a house, a
griffin would be so inconvenient: people would be continually
treading on its tail. My own idea is that what the Germans are
trying for is a mermaid, which they will then train to catch fish.

For your German does not encourage laziness in any living
thing. He likes to see his dogs work, and the German dog loves
work; of that there can be no doubt. The life of the English dog
must be a misery to him. Imagine a strong, active, and intelligent being, of exceptionally energetic temperament, condemned
to spend twenty-four hours a day in absolute idleness! How
would you like it yourself? No wonder he feels misunderstood,
yearns for the unattainable, and gets himself into trouble
generally.

Now the German dog, on the other hand, has plenty to occupy
his mind. He is busy and important. Watch him as he walks

along harnessed to his milk-cart.   No churchwarden at collection
time could feel or look more pleased with himself.   He does not
do any real work; the human being does the pushing, he does the
barking; that is his idea of division of labour.   What he says to
himself is:

'The old man can't bark, but he can shove.   Very well.'

The interest and the pride he takes in the business is quite
beautiful to see.   Another dog passing by makes, maybe, some
jeering remark, casting discredit upon the creaminess of the
milk.   He stops suddenly, quite regardless of the traffic.

'I beg your pardon, what was that you said about our milk?'

'I said nothing about your milk,' retorts the other dog, in a
tone of gentle innocence.   'I merely said it was a fine day, and
asked the price of chalk.'

'Oh, you asked the price of chalk, did you?   Would you like
to know?'

'Yes, thanks; somehow I thought you would be able to tell
me.'

'You are quite right, I can.   It's worth——'

'Oh, do come along!' says the old lady, who is tired and hot,
and anxious to finish her round.

'Yes, but hang it all, did you hear what he hinted about our
milk?'

'Oh, never mind him!   There's a tram coming round the
corner: we shall all get run over.'

'Yes, but I do mind him; one has one's proper pride.   He
asked the price of chalk, and he's going to know it!   It's worth
just twenty times as much——'

'You'll have the whole thing over, I know you will,' cries the
old lady, pathetically, struggling with all her feeble strength to
haul him back.   'Oh dear, oh dear!   I do wish I had left you
at home.'

The tram is bearing down upon them; a cab-driver is shouting
at them; another huge brute, hoping to be in time to take a hand,
is dragging a bread-cart, followed by a screaming child, across
the road from the opposite side; a small crowd is collecting;
and a policeman is hastening to the scene.

'It's worth,' says the milk dog, 'just twenty times as much as
you'll be worth before I've done with you.'

'Oh, you think so, do you?'

'Yes, I do, you grandson of a French poodle, you cabbage-
eating——'

'There! I knew you'd have it over,' says the poor milk-woman. 'I told him he'd have it over.'

But he is busy, and heeds her not. Five minutes later, when the traffic is renewed, when the bread girl has collected her muddy rolls, and the policeman has gone off with the name and address of everybody in the street, he consents to look behind him.

'It *is* a bit of an upset,' he admits. Then shaking himself free of care, he adds cheerfully: 'But I guess I taught him the price of chalk. He won't interfere with us again, I'm thinking.'

'I'm sure I hope not,' says the old lady, regarding dejectedly the milky road.

But his favourite sport is to wait at the top of the hill for another dog, and then race down. On these occasions the chief occupation of the other fellow is to run about behind, picking up the scattered articles, loaves, cabbages, or shirts, as they are jerked out. At the bottom of the hill, he stops and waits for his friend.

'Good race, wasn't it?' he remarks, panting, as the Human comes up, laden to the chin. 'I believe I'd have won it, too, if it hadn't been for that fool of a small boy. He was right in my way just as I turned the corner. *You noticed him?* Wish I had, beastly brat! What's he yelling like that for? *Because I knocked him down and ran over him?* Well, why didn't he get out of the way? It's disgraceful, the way people leave their children about for other people to tumble over. Hallo! did all those things come out? You couldn't have packed them very carefully; you should see to a thing like that. *You did not dream of my tearing down the hill twenty miles an hour?* Surely you knew me better than to expect I'd let that old Schneider's dog pass me without an effort. But there, you never think. You're sure you've got them all? *You believe so?* I shouldn't "believe" if I were you; I should run back up the hill again and make sure. *You feel too tired?* Oh, all right! don't blame me if anything is missing, that's all.'

He is so self-willed. He is cock-sure that the correct turning is the second on the right, and nothing will persuade him that it is the third. He is positive he can get across the road in time, and will not be convinced until he sees the cart smashed up. Then he is very apologetic, it is true. But of what use is that? As he is usually of the size and strength of a young bull, and his human companion is generally a weak-kneed old man or woman, or a

small child, he has his way.   The greatest punishment his proprietor can inflict upon him is to leave him at home, and take the
cart out alone.   But your German is too kind-hearted to do
this often.

That he is harnessed to the cart for anybody's pleasure but his
own it is impossible to believe; and I am confident that the German peasant plans the tiny harness and fashions the little cart
purely with the hope of gratifying his dog.   In other countries—
in Belgium, Holland, and France—I have seen these draught
dogs ill-treated and overworked; but in Germany, never.   Germans abuse animals shockingly.   I have seen a German stand in
front of his horse and call it every name he could lay his tongue
to.   But the horse did not mind it.   I have seen a German,
weary with abusing his horse, call to his wife to come out and
assist him.   When she came, he told her what the horse had
done.   The recital roused the woman's temper to almost equal
heat with his own; and standing one each side of the poor
beast, they both abused it.   They abused its dead mother, they
insulted its father; they made cutting remarks about its personal
appearance, its intelligence, its moral sense, its general ability as a
horse.   The animal bore the torrent with exemplary patience
for a while; then it did the best thing possible to do under the
circumstances.   Without losing its own temper, it moved quietly
away.   The lady returned to her washing, and the man followed
it up the street, still abusing it.

A kinder-hearted people than the Germans there is no need
for.   Cruelty to animal or child is a thing almost unknown in the
land.   The whip with them is a musical instrument; its crack is
heard from morning to night, but an Italian coachman that in the
streets of Dresden I once saw use it was very nearly lynched by
the indignant crowd.   Germany is the only country in Europe
where the traveller can settle himself comfortably in his hired
carriage, confident that his gentle, willing friend between the
shafts will be neither overworked nor cruelly treated.

CHAPTER XI

THERE was one night when, tired out and far from town or village, we slept in a Black Forest farmhouse. The great charm about the Black Forest house is its sociability. The cows are in the next room, the horses are upstairs, the geese and ducks are in the kitchen, while the pigs, the children, and the chickens live all over the place.

You are dressing, when you hear a grunt behind you.

'Good morning! Don't happen to have any potato peelings in here? No, I see you haven't; good-bye.'

Next there is a cackle, and you see the neck of an old hen stretched round the corner.

'Fine morning, isn't it? You don't mind my bringing this worm of mine in here, do you? It is so difficult in this house to find a room where one can enjoy one's food with any quietness. From a chicken I have always been a slow eater, and when a dozen—there, I thought they wouldn't leave me alone. Now they'll all want a bit. You don't mind my getting on the bed, do you? Perhaps here they won't notice me.'

While you are dressing various shock heads peer in at the door; they evidently regard the room as a temporary menagerie. You cannot tell whether the heads belong to boys or girls; you can only hope they are all male. It is of no use shutting the door, because there is nothing to fasten it by, and the moment you are gone they push it open again. You breakfast as the Prodigal Son is generally represented feeding: a pig or two drop in to keep you company; a party of elderly geese criticize you from the door; you gather from their whispers, added to their shocked expression, that they are talking scandal about you. Maybe a cow will condescend to give a glance in.

This Noah's Ark arrangement it is, I suppose, that gives to the Black Forest home its distinctive scent.   It is not a scent you can liken to any one thing.   It is as if you took roses and Limburger cheese and hair oil, some heather and onions, peaches and soap-suds, together with a dash of sea air and a corpse, and mixed them up together.   You cannot define any particular odour, but you feel they are all there—all the odours that the world has yet discovered.   People who live in these houses are fond of this mixture.   They do not open the window and lose any of it; they keep it carefully bottled up.   If you want any other scent, you can go outside and smell the wood violets and the pines: inside there is the house; and after a while, I am told, you get used to it, so that you miss it, and are unable to go to sleep in any other atmosphere.

We had a long walk before us the next day, and it was our desire, therefore, to get up early, even so early as six o'clock, if that could be managed without disturbing the whole household. We put it to our hostess whether she thought this could be done. She said she thought it could.   She might not be about herself at that time; it was her morning for going into the town, some eight miles off, and she rarely got back much before seven; but, possibly, her husband or one of the boys would be returning home to lunch about that hour.   Anyhow, somebody should be sent back to wake us and get our breakfast.

As it turned out, we did not need any waking.   We got up at four, all by ourselves.   We got up at four in order to get away from the noise and the din that was making our heads ache. What time the Black Forest peasant rises in the summer time I am unable to say; to us they appeared to be getting up all night. And the first thing the Black Forester does when he gets up is to put on a pair of stout boots with wooden soles, and take a consti-tutional round the house.   Until he has been three times up and down the stairs, he does not feel he is up.   Once fully awake himself, the next thing he does is to go upstairs to the stables, and wake up a horse.   (The Black Forest house being built generally on the side of a steep hill, the ground floor is at the top, and the hay-loft at the bottom.)   Then the horse, it would seem, must also have its constitutional round the house; and this seen to, the man goes downstairs into the kitchen and begins to chop wood, and when he has chopped sufficient wood he feels pleased with himself and begins to sing.   All things considered, we came to the conclusion we could not do better than follow the excellent example set us. Even George was quite eager to get up that morning.

We had a frugal breakfast at half past four, and started away at five. Our road lay over a mountain, and from inquiries made in the village it appeared to be one of those roads you cannot possibly miss. I suppose everybody knows this sort of road. Generally, it leads you back to where you started from; and when it doesn't, you wish it did, so that at all events you might know where you were. I foresaw evil from the very first, and before we had accomplished a couple of miles we came up with it. The road divided into three. A wormeaten signpost indicated that the path to the left led to a place that we had never heard of— that was on no map. Its other arm, pointing out the direction of the middle road, had disappeared. The road to the right, so we all agreed, clearly led back again to the village.

'The old man said distinctly,' so Harris reminded us, 'keep straight on round the hill.'

'Which hill?' George asked pertinently.

We were confronted by half a dozen, some of them big, some of them little.

'He told us,' continued Harris, 'that we should come to a wood.'

'I see no reason to doubt him,' commented George, 'whichever road we take.'

As a matter of fact, a dense wood covered every hill.

'And he said,' murmured Harris, 'that we should reach the top in about an hour and a half.'

'There it is,' said George, 'that I begin to disbelieve him.'

'Well, what shall we do?' said Harris.

Now I happen to possess the bump of locality. It is not a virtue; I make no boast of it. It is merely an animal instinct that I cannot help. That things occasionally get in my way—mountains, precipices, rivers, and such like obstructions—is no fault of mine. My instinct is correct enough; it is the earth that is wrong. I led them by the middle road. That the middle road had not character enough to continue for any quarter of a mile in the same direction; that after three miles up and down hill it ended abruptly in a wasps' nest, was not a thing that should have been laid to my door. If the middle road had gone in the direction it ought to have done, it would have taken us to where we wanted to go, of that I am convinced.

Even as it was, I would have continued to use this gift of mine to discover a fresh way had a proper spirit been displayed towards me. But I am not an angel—I admit this frankly—and I decline to exert myself for the ungrateful and the ribald. Besides, I doubt if George and Harris would have followed me farther in any event. Therefore it was that I washed my hands of the whole affair, and that Harris entered upon the vacancy.

'Well,' said Harris, 'I suppose you are satisfied with what you have done?'

'I am quite satisfied,' I replied from the heap of stones where I was sitting. 'So far, I have brought you with safety. I would continue to lead you farther, but no artist can work without encouragement. You appear dissatisfied with me because you do not know where you are. For all you know, you may be just where you want to be. But I say nothing as to that; I expect no thanks. Go your own way; I have done with you both.'

I spoke, perhaps, with bitterness, but I could not help it. Not a word of kindness had I had all the weary way.

'Do not misunderstand us,' said Harris; 'both George and myself feel that without your assistance we should never be where we now are. For that we give you every credit. But instinct is liable to error. What I propose to do is to substitute for it Science, which is exact. Now, where's the sun?'

'Don't you think,' said George, 'that if we made our way back to the village, and hired a boy for a mark to guide us, it would save time in the end?'

'It would be wasting hours,' said Harris, with decision. 'You leave this to me. I have been reading about this thing, and it has interested me.' He took out his watch, and began turning himself round and round.

'It's as simple as ABC,' he continued. 'You point the short hand at the sun, then you bisect the segment between the short hand and the twelve, and thus you get the north.'

He worried up and down for a while, then he fixed it.

'Now I've got it,' he said; 'that's the north—where that wasps' nest is. Now give me the map.'

We handed it to him and, seating himself facing the wasps, he examined it.

'Todtmoos from here,' he said, 'is south by south-west.'

'How do you mean, from here?' asked George.

'Why, from here, where we are,' returned Harris.

'But where are we?' said George.

This worried Harris for a time, but at length he cheered up.

'It doesn't matter where we are,' he said. 'Wherever we are, Todtmoos is south by south-west. Come on, we are only wasting time.'

'I don't quite see how you make it out,' said George, as he rose and shouldered his knapsack; 'but I suppose it doesn't matter. We are out for our health, and it's all pretty!'

'We shall be all right,' said Harris, with cheery confidence. 'We shall be in at Todtmoos before ten, don't you worry. And at Todtmoos we will have something to eat.'

He said that he, himself, fancied a beefsteak, followed by an omelette. George said that, personally, he intended to keep his mind off the subject until he saw Todtmoos.

We walked for half an hour, then emerging upon an opening, we saw below us, about two miles away, the village through which we had passed that morning. It had a quaint church with an outside staircase, a somewhat unusual arrangement.

The sight of it made me sad. We had been walking hard for three hours and a half, and had accomplished, apparently, about four miles. But Harris was delighted.

'Now, at last,' said Harris, 'we know where we are.'

'I thought you said it didn't matter,' George reminded him.

'No more it does, practically,' replied Harris, 'but it is just as well to be certain. Now I feel more confidence in myself.'

'I'm not so sure about that being an advantage,' muttered George. But I do not think Harris heard him.

'We are now,' continued Harris, 'east of the sun, and Todtmoos is south-west of where we are. So that if——'

He broke off. 'By the by,' he said, 'do you remember whether I said the bisecting line of that segment pointed to the north or to the south?'

'You said it pointed to the north,' replied George.

'Are you positive?' persisted Harris.

'Positive,' answered George; 'but don't let that influence your calculations. In all probability you were wrong.'

Harris thought for a while; then his brow cleared.

'That's all right,' he said; 'of course, it's the north. It must be the north. How could it be the south? Now we must make for the west. Come on.'

'I am quite willing to make for the west,' said George; 'any point of the compass is the same to me. I only wish to remark that, at the present moment, we are going dead east.'

'No, we are not,' returned Harris; 'we are going west.'

'We are going east, I tell you,' said George.

'I wish you wouldn't keep saying that,' said Harris; 'you confuse me.'

'I don't mind if I do,' returned George; 'I would rather do that than go wrong. I tell you we are going dead east.'

'What nonsense,' retorted Harris; 'there's the sun!'

'I can see the sun,' answered George, 'quite distinctly. It may be where it ought to be, according to you and Science, or it may not. All I know is, that when we were down in the village, that particular hill with that particular lump of rock upon it was due north of us. At the present moment we are facing due east.'

'You are quite right,' said Harris; 'I forgot for the moment that we had turned round.'

'I should get into the habit of making a note of it, if I were you,' grumbled George; 'it's a manœuvre that will probably occur again more than once.'

We faced about, and walked in the other direction. At the end of forty minutes' climbing we again emerged upon an opening, and again the village lay just under our feet. On this occasion it was south of us.

'This is very extraordinary,' said Harris.

'I see nothing remarkable about it,' said George. 'If you walk steadily round a village it is only natural that now and then you get a glimpse of it. Myself, I am glad to see it. It proves to me that we are not utterly lost.'

'It ought to be the other side of us,' said Harris.

'It will be in another hour or so,' said George, 'if we keep on.'

I said little myself; I was vexed with both of them; but I was glad to notice George evidently growing cross with Harris. It was absurd of Harris to fancy he could find the way by the sun.

'I wish I knew,' said Harris thoughtfully, 'for certain whether that bisecting line points to the north or to the south.'

'I should make up my mind about it,' said George; 'it's an important point.'

'It's impossible it can be the north,' said Harris, 'and I'll tell you why.'

'You needn't trouble,' said George; 'I am quite prepared to believe it isn't.'

'You said just now it was,' said Harris reproachfully.

'I said nothing of the sort,' retorted George. 'I said you said it was—a very different thing. If you think it isn't, let's go the other way. It'll be a change, at all events.'

So Harris worked things out according to the contrary calcula-
tion, and again we plunged into the wood; and again after half an
hour's stiff climbing we came in view of that same village. True,
we were a little higher, and this time it lay between us and the
sun.

'I think,' said George, as he stood looking down at it, 'this is
the best view we've had of it, as yet. There is only one other
point from which we can see it. After that, I propose we go
down into it and get some rest.'

'I don't believe it's the same village,' said Harris; 'it can't be.'

'There's no mistaking that church,' said George. 'But
maybe it is a case on all fours with that Prague statue. Possibly,
the authorities hereabout have had some life-sized models
of that village, and have stuck them about the Forest to see where
the thing would look best. Anyhow, which way do we go now?'

'I don't know,' said Harris, 'and I don't care. I have done
my best; you've done nothing but grumble, and confuse me.'

'I may have been critical,' admitted George; 'but look at the
thing from my point of view. One of you says he's got an
instinct, and leads me to a wasps' nest in the middle of a wood.'

'I can't help wasps building in a wood,' I replied.

'I don't say you can,' answered George, 'I am not arguing;
I am merely stating incontrovertible facts. The other one, who
leads me up and down hill for hours on scientific principles,
doesn't know the north from the south, and is never quite sure
whether he's turned round or whether he hasn't. Personally, I
profess to no instincts beyond the ordinary, nor am I a scientist.
But two fields off I can see a man. I am going to offer him the
worth of the hay he is cutting, which I estimate at one mark fifty
pfennig, to leave his work, and lead me to within sight of Todtmoos. If you two fellows like to follow, you can. If not, you
can start another system and work it out by yourselves.'

George's plan lacked both originality and aplomb, but at the
moment it appealed to us. Fortunately, we had worked round
to a very short distance away from the spot where we had
originally gone wrong; with the result that, aided by the gentleman of the scythe, we recovered the road, and reached Todtmoos
four hours later than we had calculated to reach it, with an
appetite that took forty-five minutes' steady work in silence to
abate.

From Todtmoos we had intended to walk down to the Rhine;
but having regard to our extra exertions of the morning, we

decided to promenade in a carriage, as the French would say; and for this purpose hired a picturesque-looking vehicle, drawn by a horse that I should have called barrel-bodied but for contrast with his driver, in comparison with whom he was angular.   In Germany every vehicle is arranged for a pair of horses, but drawn generally by one.   This gives to the equipage a lop-sided appearance, according to our notions, but it is held here to indicate style.   The idea to be conveyed is that you usually drive a pair of horses, but that for the moment you have mislaid the other one.   The German driver is not what we should call a first-class whip.   He is at his best when he is asleep.   Then, at all events, he is harmless; and the horse being, generally speaking, intelligent and experienced, progress under these conditions is comparatively safe.   If in Germany they could only train the horse to collect the money at the end of the journey, there would be no need for a coachman at all.   This would be a distinct relief to the passenger, for when the German coachman is awake and not cracking his whip he is generally occupied in getting himself into trouble or out of it.   He is better at the former.   Once I recollect driving down a steep Black Forest hill with a couple of ladies.   It was one of those roads winding corkscrew-wise down the slope.   The hill rose at an angle of seventy-five on the offside, and fell away at an angle of seventy-five on the nearside. We were proceeding very comfortably, the driver, we were happy to notice, with his eyes shut, when suddenly something, a bad dream or indigestion, awoke him.   He seized the reins, and, by an adroit movement, pulled the nearside horse over the edge, where it clung, half-supported by the traces.   Our driver did not appear in the least annoyed or surprised; both horses, I also noticed, seemed equally used to the situation.   We got out, and he got down.   He took from under the seat a huge clasp-knife, evidently kept there for the purpose, and deftly cut the traces. The horse, thus released rolled over and over until it struck the road again some fifty feet below.   There he regained his feet and stood waiting for us.   We re-entered the carriage and descended with the single horse until we came to him.   There, with the help of some bits of string, our driver harnessed him again, and we continued on our way.   What impressed me was the evident accustomedness of both driver and horses to this method of working down a hill.

Evidently to them it appeared a short and convenient cut.   I should not have been surprised had the man suggested our strapping ourselves in, and then rolling over and over, carriage and all, to the bottom.

Another peculiarity of the German coachman is that he never attempts to pull in or to pull up. He regulates his rate of speed, not by the pace of the horse, but by manipulation of the brake. For eight miles an hour he puts it on slightly, so that it only scrapes the wheel, producing a continuous sound as of the sharpening of a saw; for four miles an hour he screws it down harder, and you travel to an accompaniment of groans and shrieks, suggestive of a symphony of dying pigs. When he desires to come to a full stop, he puts it on to its full. If his brake be a good one, he calculates he can stop his carriage, unless the horse be an extra powerful animal, in less than twice its own length. Neither the German driver nor the German horse knows, apparently, that you can stop a carriage by any other method. The German horse continues to pull with his full strength until he finds it impossible to move the vehicle another inch; then he rests. Horses of other countries are quite willing to stop when the idea is suggested to them. I have known horses content to go even quite slowly. But your German horse, seemingly, is built for one particular speed, and is unable to depart from it. I am stating nothing but the literal, unadorned truth, when I say I have seen a German coachman, with the reins lying loose over the splash-board, working his brake with both hands, in terror lest he would not be in time to avoid a collision.

At Waldshut, one of those little sixteenth-century towns through which the Rhine flows during its earlier course, we came across that exceedingly common object of the Continent: the travelling Briton grieved and surprised at the unacquaintance of the foreigner with the subtleties of the English language. When we entered the station he was, in very fair English, though with a slight Somersetshire accent, explaining to a porter for the tenth time, as he informed us, the simple fact that though he himself had a ticket for Donaueschingen, and wanted to go to Donaueschingen, to see the source of the Danube, which is not there, though they tell you it is, he wished his bicycle to be sent on to Engen and his bag to Constance, there to await his arrival. He was hot and angry with the effort of the thing. The porter was a young man in years, but at the moment looked old and miserable. I offered my services. I wish now I had not—though not so fervently, I expect, as he, the speechless one, came subsequently to wish this. All three routes, so the porter explained to

us, were complicated, necessitating changing and rechanging.
There was not much time for calm elucidation, as our own train
was starting in a few minutes.   The man himself was voluble—
always a mistake when anything entangled has to be made clear;

Explaining to the porter

while the porter was only too eager to get the job done with and
so breathe again.   It dawned upon me ten minutes later, when
thinking the matter over in the train, that though I had agreed
with the porter that it would be best for the bicycle to go by way of
Immendingen, and had agreed to his booking it to Immendingen,
I had neglected to give instructions for its departure from

Immendingen.   Were I of a despondent temperament I should
be worrying myself at the present moment with the reflection
that in all probability that bicycle is still at Immendingen to this
day.   But I regard it as good philosophy to endeavour always to
see the brighter side of things.   Possibly the porter corrected my
omission on his own account, or some simple miracle may have
happened to restore that bicycle to its owner some time before
the end of his tour.   The bag we sent to Radolfzell: but here I
console myself with the recollection that it was labelled Constance; and no doubt after a while the railway authorities, finding
it unclaimed at Radolfzell, forwarded it on to Constance.

But all this is apart from the moral I wished to draw from the
incident.   The true inwardness of the situation lay in the
indignation of this Britisher at finding a German railway porter
unable to comprehend English.   The moment we spoke to him
he expressed this indignation in no measured terms.

'Thank you, very much indeed,' he said; 'it's simple enough.
I want to go to Donaueschingen myself by train; from Donaueschingen I am going to walk to Geisengen; from Geisengen I
am going to take the train to Engen; and from Engen I am going
to bicycle to Constance.   But I don't want to take my bag with
me; I want to find it at Constance when I get there.   I have
been trying to explain the thing to this fool for the last ten
minutes; but I can't get it into him.'

'It is very disgraceful,' I agreed.   'Some of these German
workmen know hardly any other language than their own.'

'I have gone over it with him,' continued the man, 'on the
time-table, and explained it by pantomime.   Even then I could
not knock it into him.'

'I can hardly believe you,' I again remarked; 'you would think
the thing explained itself.'

Harris was angry with the man; he wished to reprove him for
his folly in journeying through the outlying portions of a foreign
clime, and seeking in such to accomplish complicated railway
tricks without knowing a word of the language of the country.
But I checked the impulsiveness of Harris, and pointed out to
him the great and good work at which the man was unconsciously
assisting.

Shakespeare and Milton may have done their little best to
spread acquaintance with the English tongue among the less
favoured inhabitants of Europe.   Newton and Darwin may have
rendered their language a necessity among educated and

thoughtful foreigners. Dickens and Ouida (for your folk who imagine that the literary world is bounded by the prejudices of New Grub Street, would be surprised and grieved at the position occupied abroad by this at-home-sneered-at-lady) may have helped still further to popularize it. But the man who has spread the knowledge of English from Cape St Vincent to the Ural Mountains is the Englishman who, unable or unwilling to learn a single word of any language but his own, travels purse in hand into every corner of the Continent. One may be shocked at his ignorance, annoyed at his stupidity, angry at his presumption. But the practical fact remains: he it is that is anglicizing Europe. For him the Swiss peasant tramps through the snow on winter evenings to attend the English class open in every village. For him the coachman and the guard, the chambermaid and the laundress, pore over their English grammars and colloquial phrase-books. For him the foreign shopkeeper and merchant send their sons and daughters in their thousands to study in every English town. For him it is that every foreign hotel- and restaurant-keeper adds to his advertisement: 'Only those with fair knowledge of English need apply.'

Did the English-speaking races make it their rule to speak anything else than English, the marvellous progress of the English tongue throughout the world would stop. The English-speaking man stands amid the strangers and jingles his gold.

'Here,' he cries, 'is payment for all such as can speak English.'

He it is who is the great educator. Theoretically we may scold him; practically we should take our hats off to him. He is the missionary of the English tongue.

CHAPTER XII

A THING that vexes much the high-class Anglo-Saxon soul is the earthly instinct prompting the German to fix a restaurant at the goal of every excursion. On mountain summit, in fairy glen, on lonely pass, by waterfall or winding stream, stands ever the busy Wirtschaft. How can one rhapsodize over a view when surrounded by beer-stained tables? How lose one's self in historical reverie amid the odour of roast veal and spinach?

One day, on elevating thoughts intent, we climbed through tangled woods.

'And at the top,' said Harris bitterly, as we paused to breathe a space and pull our belts a hole tighter, 'there will be a gaudy restaurant, where people will be guzzling beefsteaks and plum tarts and drinking white wine.'

'Do you think so?' said George.

'Sure to be,' answered Harris; 'you know their way. Not one grove will they consent to dedicate to solitude and contemplation; not one height will they leave to the lover of nature unpolluted by the gross and the material.'

'I calculate,' I remarked, 'that we shall be there a little before one o'clock, provided we don't dawdle.'

'The *mittagstisch* will be just ready,' groaned Harris, 'with possibly some of those little blue trout they catch about here. In Germany one never seems able to get away from food and drink. It is maddening!'

We pushed on, and in the beauty of the walk forgot our indignation. My estimate proved to be correct.

At a quarter to one, said Harris, who was leading:

'Here we are; I can see the summit.'

'Any sign of that restaurant?' said George.

'I don't notice it,' replied Harris; 'but it's there, you may be sure; confound it!'

Five minutes later we stood upon the top. We looked north, south, east, and west; then we looked at one another.

'Grand view, isn't it?' said Harris.

'Magnificent,' I agreed.

'Superb,' remarked George.

'They have had the good sense for once,' said Harris, 'to put that restaurant out of sight.'

'They do seem to have hidden it,' said George.

'One doesn't mind the thing so much when it is not forced under one's nose,' said Harris.

'Of course, in its place,' I observed, 'a restaurant is right enough.'

'I should like to know where they have put it,' said George.

'Suppose we look for it?' said Harris with inspiration.

It seemed a good idea. I felt curious myself. We agreed to explore in different directions, returning to the summit to report progress. In half an hour we stood together once again. There was no need for words. The face of one and all of us announced plainly that at last we had discovered a recess of German nature untarnished by the sordid suggestion of food or drink.

'I should never have believed it possible,' said Harris, 'would you?'

'I should say,' I replied, 'that this is the only square quarter of a mile in the entire Fatherland unprovided with one.'

'And we three strangers have struck it,' said George, 'without an effort.'

'True,' I observed. 'By pure good fortune we are now enabled to feast our finer senses undisturbed by appeal to our lower nature. Observe the light upon those distant peaks; is it not ravishing?'

'Talking of nature,' said George, 'which should you say was the nearest way down?'

'The road to the left,' I replied, after consulting the guide-book, 'takes us to Sonnensteig—where, by the by, I observe the Goldener Adler is well spoken of—in about two hours. The road to the right, though somewhat longer, commands more extensive prospects.'

'One prospect,' said Harris, 'is very much like another prospect; don't you think so?'

'Personally,' said George, 'I am going by the left-hand road.'
And Harris and I went after him.

But we were not to get down so soon as we had anticipated.
Storms come quickly in these regions, and before we had walked
for a quarter of an hour it became a question of seeking shelter or
living for the rest of the day in soaked clothes. We decided on
the former alternative, and selected a tree that, under ordinary
circumstances, should have been ample protection. But a Black
Forest thunderstorm is not an ordinary circumstance. We consoled ourselves at first by telling each other that at such a rate it
could not last long. Next, we endeavoured to comfort ourselves
with the reflection that if it did we should soon be too wet to fear
getting wetter.

'As it turned out,' said Harris, 'I should have been almost glad
if there had been a restaurant up here.'

'I see no advantage in being both wet *and* hungry,' said George.
'I shall give it another five minutes, then I am going on.'

'These mountain solitudes,' I remarked, 'are very attractive
in fine weather. On a rainy day, especially if you happen to be
past the age when——'

At this point there hailed us a voice, proceeding from a stout
gentleman, who stood some fifty feet away from us under a big
umbrella.

'Won't you come inside?' asked the stout gentleman.

'Inside where?' I called back. I thought at first he was one
of those fools that will try to be funny when there is nothing to be
funny about.

'Inside the restaurant,' he answered.

We left our shelter and made for him. We wished for further
information about this thing.

'I did call to you from the window,' said the stout gentleman,
as we drew near to him, 'but I suppose you did not hear me.
This storm may last for another hour; you will get *so* wet.'

He was a kindly old gentleman; he seemed quite anxious
about us.

I said: 'It is very kind of you to have come out. We are not
lunatics. We have not been standing under that tree for the last
half-hour knowing all the time there was a restaurant, hidden by
the trees, within twenty yards of us. We had no idea we were
anywhere near a restaurant.'

'I thought maybe you hadn't,' said the old gentleman; 'that
is why I came.'

It appeared that all the people in the inn had been watching us from the windows also, wondering why we stood there looking miserable. If it had not been for this nice old gentleman the fools would have remained watching us, I suppose, for the rest of the afternoon. The landlord excused himself by saying he thought we looked like English. It is no figure of speech. On the Continent they do sincerely believe that every Englishman is mad. They are as convinced of it as is every English peasant that Frenchmen live on frogs. Even when one makes a direct personal effort to disabuse them of the impression one is not always successful.

It was a comfortable little restaurant, where they cooked well, while the *Tischwein* was really most passable. We stopped there for a couple of hours, and dried ourselves and fed ourselves, and talked about the view; and just before we left an incident occurred that shows how much more stirring in this world are the influences of evil compared with those of good.

A traveller entered. He seemed a careworn man. He carried a brick in his hand tied to a piece of rope. He entered nervously and hurriedly, closed the door carefully behind him, saw to it that it was fastened, peered out of the window long and earnestly, and then, with a sigh of relief, laid his brick upon the bench beside him and called for food and drink.

There was something mysterious about the whole affair. One wondered what he was going to do with the brick, why he had

A brick . . . tied to a rope

closed the door so carefully, why he had looked so anxiously from the window; but his aspect was too wretched to invite conversation, and we forbore, therefore, to ask him questions. As he ate and drank he grew more cheerful, sighed less often. Later he stretched his legs, lit an evil-smelling cigar, and puffed in calm contentment.

Then it happened. It happened too suddenly for any detailed explanation of the thing to be possible. I recollect a fraulein entering the room from the kitchen with a pan in her hand. I saw her cross to the outer door. The next moment the whole room was in an uproar. One was reminded of those pantomime transformation scenes where, from among floating clouds, slow music, waving flowers, and reclining fairies, one is suddenly transported into the midst of shouting policemen tumbling over yelling babies, swells fighting pantaloons, sausages and harle-quins, buttered slides and clowns. As the fraulein of the pan touched the door it flew open, as though all the spirits of sin had been pressed against it, waiting. Two pigs and a chicken rushed into the room; a cat that had been sleeping on a beer-barrel spluttered into fiery life. The fraulein threw her pan into the air and lay down on the floor. The gentleman with the brick sprang to his feet, upsetting the table before him with everything upon it.

One looked to see the cause of this disaster: one discovered it at once in the person of a mongrel terrier with pointed ears and a squirrel's tail. The landlord rushed out from another door, and attempted to kick him out of the room. Instead, he kicked one of the pigs, the fatter of the two. It was a vigorous, well-planted kick, and the pig got the whole of it; none of it was wasted. One felt sorry for the poor animal; but no amount of sorrow anyone else might feel for him could compare with the sorrow he felt for himself. He stopped running about; he sat down in the middle of the room, and appealed to the solar system generally to observe this unjust thing that had come upon him. They must have heard his complaint in the valleys round about, and have wondered what upheaval of nature was taking place among the hills.

As for the hen it scuttled, screaming, every way at once. It was a marvellous bird: it seemed to be able to run up a straight wall quite easily; and it and the cat between them fetched down mostly everything that was not already on the floor. In less than forty seconds there were nine people in that room, all trying to kick one dog. Possibly, now and again, one or another may have succeeded, for occasionally the dog would stop barking in order to howl. But it did not discourage him. Everything has to be paid for, he evidently argued, even a pig and chicken hunt; and, on the whole, the game was worth it.

Besides, he had the satisfaction of observing that, for every kick he received, most other living things in the room got two. As for the unfortunate pig—the stationary one, the one that still sat lamenting in the centre of the room—he must have averaged a steady four. Trying to kick this dog was like playing football with a ball that was never there—not when you went to kick it, but after you had started to kick it, and had gone too far to stop yourself, so that the kick had to go on in any case, your only hope being that your foot would find something or another solid to stop it, and so save you from sitting down on the floor noisily and completely. When anybody did kick the dog it was by pure accident, when they were not expecting to kick him; and, generally speaking, this took them so unawares that, after kicking him, they fell over him. And everybody, every half-minute, would be certain to fall over the pig, the sitting pig, the one incapable of getting out of anybody's way.

How long the scrimmage might have lasted it is impossible to say. It was ended by the judgment of George. For a while he had been seeking to catch, not the dog but the remaining pig, the one still capable of activity. Cornering it at last, he persuaded it to cease running round and round the room, and instead to take a spin outside. It shot through the door with one long wail.

We always desire the thing we have not. One pig, a chicken, nine people, and a cat, were as nothing in that dog's opinion compared with the quarry that was disappearing. Unwisely, he darted after it, and George closed the door upon him and shot the bolt.

Then the landlord stood up, and surveyed all the things that were lying on the floor.

'That's a playful dog of yours,' said he to the man who had come in with the brick.

'He is not my dog,' replied the man sullenly.

'Whose dog is it then?' said the landlord.

'I don't know whose dog it is,' answered the man.

'That won't do for me, you know,' said the landlord, picking up a picture of the German Emperor, and wiping beer from it with his sleeve.

'I know it won't,' replied the man; 'I never expected it would. I'm tired of telling people it isn't my dog. They none of them believe me.'

'What do you want to go about with him for, if he's not your dog?' said the landlord. 'What's the attraction about him?'

'I don't go about with him,' replied the man; 'he goes about with me. He picked me up this morning at ten o'clock, and he won't leave me. I thought I had got rid of him when I came in here. I left him busy killing a duck more than a quarter of an hour away. I'll have to pay for that, I expect, on my way back.'

'Have you tried throwing stones at him?' asked Harris.

'Have I tried throwing stones at him!' replied the man, contemptuously. 'I've been throwing stones at him till my arm aches with throwing stones; and he thinks it's a game, and brings them back to me. I've been carrying this beastly brick about with me for over an hour, in the hope of being able to drown him, but he never comes near enough for me to get hold of him. He just sits six inches out of reach with his mouth open, and looks at me.'

'It's the funniest story I've heard for a long while,' said the landlord.

'Glad it amuses somebody,' said the man.

We left him helping the landlord to pick up the broken things, and went our way. A dozen yards outside the door the faithful animal was waiting for his friend. He looked tired, but contented. He was evidently a dog of strange and sudden fancies, and we feared for the moment lest he might take a liking to us. But he let us pass with indifference. His loyalty to this unresponsive man was touching; and we made no attempt to undermine it.

Having completed to our satisfaction the Black Forest, we journeyed on our wheels through Alt Breisach and Colmar to Münster; whence we started a short exploration of the Vosges range, where according to the present German Emperor, humanity stops. Of old, Alt Breisach, a rocky fortress with the river now on one side of it and now on the other—for in its inexperienced youth the Rhine never seems to have been quite sure of its way—must, as a place of residence, have appealed exclusively to the lover of change and excitement. Whoever the war was between, and whatever it was about, Alt Breisach was bound to be in it. Everybody besieged it, most people captured it; the majority of them lost it again; nobody seemed able to keep it. Whom he belonged to, and what he was, the dweller in Alt Breisach could never have been quite sure. One day he would be a Frenchman, and then before he could learn enough French to pay his taxes he would be an Austrian. While trying to discover what you did in order to be a good Austrian, he would find he was no longer an Austrian, but a German, though what particular German out of the dozen must always have been

doubtful to him. One day he would discover that he was a
Catholic, the next an ardent Protestant. The only thing that
could have given any stability to his existence must have been the
monotonous necessity of paying heavily for the privilege of being
whatever for the moment he was. But when one begins to think
of these things one finds oneself wondering why anybody in the
Middle Ages, except kings and tax collectors, ever took the
trouble to live at all.

For variety and beauty, the Vosges will not compare with the
hills of the Schwarzwald. The advantage about them from the
tourist's point of view is their superior poverty. The Vosges
peasant has not the unromantic air of contented prosperity that
spoils his vis-à-vis across the Rhine. The villages and farms
possess more the charm of decay. Another point wherein the
Vosges district excels is its ruins. Many of its numerous castles
are perched where you might think only eagles would care to
build. In others, commenced by the Romans and finished by
the Troubadours, covering acres with the maze of their still
standing walls, one may wander for hours.

The fruiterer and greengrocer is a person unknown in the
Vosges. Most things of that kind grow wild, and are to be had
for the picking. It is difficult to keep to any programme when
walking through the Vosges, the temptation on a hot day to stop
and eat fruit generally being too strong for resistance. Raspberries, the most delicious I have ever tasted, wild strawberries,
currants, and gooseberries, grow upon the hillsides as blackberries by English lanes. The Vosges small boy is not called
upon to rob an orchard; he can make himself ill without sin.
Orchards exist in the Vosges mountains in plenty; but to trespass
into one for the purpose of stealing fruit would be as foolish as for
a fish to try and get into a swimming-bath without paying. Still,
of course, mistakes do occur.

One afternoon in the course of a climb we emerged upon a
plateau, where we lingered perhaps too long, eating more fruit
than may have been good for us; it was so plentiful around us,
so varied. We commenced with a few late strawberries, and
from those we passed to raspberries. Then Harris found a
greengage-tree with some early fruit upon it, just perfect.

'This is about the best thing we have struck,' said George;
'we had better make the most of this.' Which was good advice,
on the face of it.

'It is a pity,' said Harris, 'that the pears are still so hard.'

He grieved about this for a while, but later on I came across some remarkably fine yellow plums and these consoled him somewhat.

'I suppose we are still a bit too far north for pineapples,' said George. 'I feel I could just enjoy a fresh pineapple. This commonplace fruit palls upon one after a while.'

'Too much bush fruit and not enough tree, is the fault I find,' said Harris. 'Myself, I should have liked a few more green-gages.'

'Here is a man coming up the hill,' I observed, 'who looks like a native. Maybe, he will know where we can find some more greengages.'

'He walks well for an old chap,' remarked Harris.

He certainly was climbing the hill at a remarkable pace. Also, so far as we were able to judge at that distance, he appeared to be in a remarkably cheerful mood, singing and shouting at the top of his voice, gesticulating, and waving his arms.

'What a merry old soul he is,' said Harris; 'it does one good to watch him. But why does he carry his stick over his shoulder? Why doesn't he use it to help him up the hill?'

'Do you know, I don't think it is a stick,' said George.

'What can it be, then?' asked Harris.

'Well, it looks to me,' said George, 'more like a gun.'

'You don't think we can have made a mistake?' suggested Harris. 'You don't think this can be anything in the nature of a private orchard?'

I said: 'Do you remember the sad thing that happened in the South of France some two years ago? A soldier picked some cherries as he passed a house, and the French peasant to whom the cherries belonged came out, and without a word of warning shot him dead.'

'But surely you are not allowed to shoot a man dead for picking fruit, even in France?' said George.

'Of course not,' I answered. 'It was quite illegal. The only excuse offered by his counsel was that he was of a highly excitable disposition, and especially keen about these particular cherries.'

'I recollect something about the case,' said Harris, 'now you mention it. I believe the district in which it happened—the "Commune," as I think it is called—had to pay heavy compensation to the relatives of the deceased soldier; which was only fair.'

George said: 'I am tired of this place. Besides, it's getting late.'

Harris said: 'If he goes at that rate he will fall and hurt himself. Besides, I don't believe he knows the way.'

I felt lonesome up there all by myself, with nobody to speak to. Besides, not since I was a boy, I reflected, had I enjoyed a run down a really steep hill. I thought I would see if I could revive the sensation. It is a jerky exercise, but good, I should say, for the liver.

We slept that night at Barr, a pleasant little town on the way to St Ottilienberg, an interesting old convent among the mountains, where you are waited upon by real nuns, and your bill made out by a priest. At Barr, just before supper a tourist entered. He looked English, but spoke a language the like of which I have never heard before. Yet it was an elegant and fine-sounding language. The landlord stared at him blankly; the landlady shook her head. He sighed, and tried another, which somehow recalled to me forgotten memories, though, at the time, I could not fix it. But again nobody understood him.

'This is damnable,' he said aloud to himself.

'Ah, you are English!' exclaimed the landlord, brightening up.

'And Monsieur looks tired,' added the bright little landlady. 'Monsieur will have supper.'

They both spoke English excellently, nearly as well as they spoke French and German; and they bustled about and made him comfortable. At supper he sat next to me, and I talked to him.

'Tell me,' I said—I was curious on the subject—'what language was it you spoke when you first came in?'

'German,' he explained.

'Oh,' I replied, 'I beg your pardon.'

'You did not understand it?' he continued.

'It must have been my fault,' I answered; 'my knowledge is extremely limited. One picks up a little here and there as one goes about, but of course that is a different thing.'

'But *they* did not understand it,' he replied, 'the landlord and his wife; and it is their own language.'

'I do not think so,' I said. 'The children hereabout speak German, it is true, and our landlord and landlady know German to a certain point. But throughout Alsace and Lorraine the old people still talk French.'

'And I spoke to them in French also,' he added, 'and they understood that no better.'

'It is certainly very curious,' I agreed.

'It is more than curious,' he replied; 'in my case it is incomprehensible. I possess a diploma for modern languages. I won my scholarship purely on the strength of my French and German. The correctness of my construction, the purity of my pronunciation, was considered at my college to be quite remarkable. Yet, when I come abroad hardly anybody understands a word I say. Can you explain it?'

'I think I can,' I replied. 'Your pronunciation is too faultless. You remember what the Scotsman said when for the first time in his life he tasted real whisky: "It may be puir, but I canna drink it"; so it is with your German. It strikes one less as a language than as an exhibition. If I might offer advice, I should say: Mispronounce as much as possible and throw in as many mistakes as you can think of.'

It is the same everywhere. Each country keeps a special pronunciation exclusively for the use of foreigners—a pronunciation they never dream of using themselves, that they cannot understand when it is used. I once heard an English lady explaining to a Frenchman how to pronounce the word 'have.'

'You will pronounce it,' said the lady reproachfully, 'as if it were spelt h-a-v. It isn't. There is an "e" at the end.'

'But I thought,' said the pupil, 'that you did not sound the "e" at the end of h-a-v-e.'

'No more you do,' explained his teacher. 'It is what we call a mute "e"; but it exercises a modifying influence on the preceding vowel.'

Before that, he used to say 'have' quite intelligently. Afterwards, when he came to the word he would stop dead, collect his thoughts, and give expression to a sound that only the context could explain.

Putting aside the sufferings of the early martyrs, few men, I suppose, have gone through more than I myself went through in trying to attain the correct pronunciation of the German word for church—*Kirche*. Long before I had done with it I had determined never to go to church in Germany, rather than be bothered with it.

'No, no,' my teacher would explain—he was a painstaking gentleman; 'you say it as if it were spelt K-i-r-c-h-k-e. There is no k. It is——' And he would illustrate to me again, for the twentieth time that morning, how it should be pronounced; the sad thing being that I could never for the life of me detect any

difference between the way he said it and the way I said it.   So
he would try a new method.

'You say it from your throat,' he would explain.   He was
quite right, I did.   'I want you to say it from down here,' and
with a fat forefinger he would indicate the region from where I
was to start.   After painful efforts, resulting in sounds suggestive
of anything rather than a place of worship, I would excuse myself.

'I really fear it is impossible,' I would say.   'You see, for
years I have always talked with my mouth, as it were; I never
knew a man could talk with his stomach.   I doubt if it is not too
late now for me to learn.'

By spending hours in dark corners, and practising in silent
streets, to the terror of chance passers-by, I came at last to pronounce this word correctly.   My teacher was delighted with me,
and until I came to Germany I was pleased with myself.   In
Germany I found that nobody understood what I meant by it.
I never got near a church with it.   I had to drop the correct
pronunciation, and painstakingly go back to my first wrong
pronunciation.   Then they would brighten up, and tell me it
was round the corner, or down the next street, as the case might
be.

I also think pronunciation of a foreign tongue could be better
taught than by demanding from the pupil those internal acrobatic
feats that are generally impossible and always useless.   This is
the sort of instruction one receives:

'Press your tonsils against the underside of your larynx.
Then with the convex part of the septum curved upwards so as
almost—but not quite—to touch the uvula, try with the tip of
your tongue to reach your thyroid.   Take a deep breath, and
compress your glottis.   Now, without opening your lips, say
"Garoo."'

And when you have done it they are not satisfied.

CHAPTER XIII

On our way home we included a German University town, being
wishful to obtain an insight into the ways of student life, a
curiosity that the courtesy of German friends enabled us to
gratify.

The English boy plays till he is fifteen, and works thence till
twenty. In Germany it is the child that works; the young man
that plays. The German boy goes to school at seven o'clock in
the summer, at eight in the winter, and at school he studies.
The result is that at sixteen he has a thorough knowledge of the
classics and mathematics, knows as much history as any man
compelled to belong to a political party is wise in knowing,
together with a thorough grounding in modern languages.
Therefore his eight College Semesters, extending over four years,
are, except for the young man aiming at a professorship, unnecessarily ample. He is not a sportsman, which is a pity, for he
should make a good one. He plays football a little, bicycles still
less; plays French billiards in stuffy cafés more. But generally
speaking he, or the majority of him, lays out his time bummeling,
beer drinking, and fighting. If he be the son of a wealthy father
he joins a Korps—to belong to a crack Korps costs about four
hundred pounds a year. If he be a middle-class young man, he
enrols himself in a Burschenschaft, or a Landsmannschaft, which
is still a little cheaper. These companies are again broken up
into smaller circles, in which attempt is made to keep to nation-
ality. There are the Swabians, from Swabia; the Frankonians,
descendants of the Franks; the Thuringians, and so forth. In
practice, of course, this results as all such attempts do result—I
believe half our Gordon Highlanders are Cockneys—but the
picturesque object is obtained of dividing each University into

some dozen or so separate companies of students, each one with its distinctive cap and colours, and, quite as important, its own particular beer hall, into which no other student wearing his colours may come.

The chief work of these student companies is to fight among themselves, or with some rival Korps or Schaft, the celebrated German Mensur.

The Mensur has been described so often and so thoroughly that I do not intend to bore my readers with any detailed account of it. I merely come forward as an impressionist, and I write purposely the impression of my first Mensur, because I believe that first impressions are more true and useful than opinions blunted by intercourse, or shaped by influence.

A Frenchman or a Spaniard will seek to persuade you that the bullring is an institution got up chiefly for the benefit of the bull. The horse which you imagined to be screaming with pain was only laughing at the comical appearance presented by its own inside. Your French or Spanish friend contrasts its glorious and exciting death in the ring with the cold-blooded brutality of the knacker's yard. If you do not keep a tight hold of your head, you come away with the desire to start an agitation for the inception of the bullring in England as an aid to chivalry. No doubt Torquemada was convinced of the humanity of the Inquisition. To a stout gentleman, suffering, perhaps, from cramp or rheumatism, an hour or so on the rack was really a physical benefit. He would rise feeling more free in his joints— more elastic, as one might say, than he had felt for years. English huntsmen regard the fox as an animal to be envied. A day's excellent sport is provided for him free of charge, during which he is the centre of attraction.

Use blinds one to everything one does not wish to see. Every third German gentleman you meet in the street still bears, and will bear to his grave, marks of the twenty to a hundred duels he has fought in his student days. The German children play at the Mensur in the nursery, rehearse it in the gymnasium. The Germans have come to persuade themselves there is no brutality in it—nothing offensive, nothing degrading. Their argument is that it schools the German youth to coolness and courage. If this could be proved, the argument, particularly in a country where every man is a soldier, would be sufficiently one-sided. But is the virtue of the prize-fighter the virtue of the soldier? One doubts it. Nerve and dash are surely of more service in the field than a temperament of unreasoning indifference as to what is happening to one. As a matter of fact, the German student would have to be possessed of much more courage not to fight. He fights not to please himself, but to satisfy a public opinion that is two hundred years behind the times.

All the Mensur does is to brutalize him. There may be skill displayed—I am told there is—but it is not apparent. The mere fighting is like nothing so much as a broadsword combat at a Richardson's show; the display as a whole a successful attempt to combine the ludicrous with the unpleasant. In aristocratic Bonn, where style is considered, and in Heidelberg, where visitors from other nations are more common, the affair is perhaps more formal. I am told that there the contests take place in handsome rooms; that grey-haired doctors wait upon the wounded, and liveried servants upon the hungry, and that the affair is conducted throughout with a certain amount of pictur-esque ceremony. In the more essentially German Universities, where strangers are rare and not much encouraged, the simple essentials are the only things kept in view, and these are not of an inviting nature.

Indeed, so distinctly uninviting are they, that I strongly advise the sensitive reader to avoid even this description of them. The subject cannot be made pretty, and I do not intend to try.

The room is bare and sordid; its walls splashed with mixed stains of beer, blood, and candle-grease; its ceiling, smoky; its floor, sawdust covered. A crowd of students, laughing, smoking, talking, some sitting on the floor, others perched upon chairs and benches, form the framework.

In the centre, facing one another, stand the combatants, resembling Japanese warriors, as made familiar to us by the Japanese tea-tray. Quaint and rigid, with their goggle-covered eyes, their necks tied up in comforters, their bodies smothered in what looks like dirty bed quilts, their padded arms stretched straight above their heads, they might be a pair of ungainly clock-work figures. The seconds, also more or less padded—their heads and faces protected by huge leather-peaked caps—drag them out into their proper position. One almost listens to hear the sound of the castors. The umpire takes his place, the word is given, and immediately there follow five rapid clashes of the long straight swords. There is no interest in watching the fight: there is no movement, no skill, no grace (I am speaking of my own impressions). The strongest man wins; the man who, with

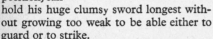

his heavily
padded arm,
always in an
unnatural
position, can
hold his huge clumsy sword longest without growing too weak to be able either to
guard or to strike.

The whole interest is centred in watching
the wounds.   They come always in one of
two places—on the top of the head or the
left side of the face.   Sometimes a portion
of hairy scalp or section of cheek flies up
into the air, to be carefully preserved in an
envelope by its proud possessor, or, strictly
speaking, its proud former possessor, and
shown round on convivial evenings; and
from every wound, of course, flows a plentiful stream of blood.   It splashes doctors,
seconds, and spectators; it sprinkles ceiling
and walls; it saturates the fighters, and
makes pools for itself in the
sawdust.   At the end of each
round the doctors rush up and,
with hands already dripping with
blood, press together the gaping
wounds, dabbing them with little

The German duellist

balls of wet cotton wool, which an attendant carries ready on a
plate.   Naturally, the moment the men stand up again and commence work, the blood gushes out again, half blinding them, and
rendering the ground beneath them slippery.   Now and then you
see a man's teeth laid bare almost to the ear, so that for the rest
of the duel he appears to be grinning at one half of the spectators,
his other side remaining serious; and sometimes a man's nose gets
slit, which gives to him as he fights a singularly supercilious air.

As the object of each student is to go away from the University
bearing as many scars as possible, I doubt if any particular pains
are taken to guard, even to the small extent such method of
fighting can allow.   The real victor is he who comes out with the
greatest number of wounds; he who then, stitched and patched
almost to unrecognition as a human being, can promenade for the
next month, the envy of the German youth, the admiration of the

German maiden. He who obtains only a few unimportant wounds retires sulky and disappointed.

But the actual fighting is only the beginning of the fun. The second act of the spectacle takes place in the dressing-room. The doctors are generally mere medical students—young fellows who, having taken their degree, are anxious for practice. Truth compels me to say that those with whom I came in contact were coarse-looking men who seemed rather to relish their work. Perhaps they are not to be blamed for this. It is part of the system that as much further punishment as possible must be inflicted by the doctor, and the ideal medical man might hardly care for such job. How the student bears the dressing of his wounds is as important as how he receives them. Every operation has to be performed as brutally as may be, and his companions carefully watch him during the process to see that he goes through it with an appearance of peace and enjoyment. A clean-cut wound that gapes wide is most desired by all parties. On purpose it is sewn up clumsily, with the hope that by this means the scar will last a lifetime. Such a wound, judiciously mauled and interfered with during the week afterwards, can generally be reckoned on to secure its fortunate possessor a wife with a dowry of five figures at the least.

These are the general bi-weekly Mensurs, of which the average student fights some dozen a year. There are others to which visitors are not admitted. When a student is considered to have disgraced himself by some slight involuntary movement of the head or body while fighting, then he can only regain his position by standing up to the best swordsman in his Korps. He demands, and is accorded, not a contest, but a punishment. His opponent then proceeds to inflict as many and as bloody wounds as can be taken. The object of the victim is to show his comrades that he can stand still while his head is half sliced from his skull.

Whether anything can properly be said in favour of the German Mensur I am doubtful; but if so it concerns only the two combatants. Upon the spectators it can and does, I am convinced, exercise nothing but evil. I know myself sufficiently well to be sure I am not of an unusually bloodthirsty disposition. The effect it had upon me can only be the usual effect. At first, before the actual work commenced, my sensation was curiosity mingled with anxiety as to how the sight would trouble me, though some slight acquaintance with dissecting-rooms and operating tables left me less doubt on that point than I might otherwise have felt. As the blood began to flow, and nerves and muscles to be laid bare, I experienced a mingling of disgust and pity. But with the second duel, I must confess, my finer feelings began to disappear; and by the time the third was well upon its way, and the room heavy with the curious hot odour of blood, I began, as the American expression is, to see things red.

I wanted more. I looked from face to face surrounding me, and in most of them I found reflected undoubtedly my own sensations. If it be a good thing to excite this blood thirst in the modern man, then the Mensur is a useful institution. But is it a good thing? We prate about our civilization and humanity, but those of us who do not carry hypocrisy to the length of self-deception know that underneath our starched shirts there lurks the savage, with all his savage instincts untouched. Occasionally he may be wanted, but we never need fear his dying out. On the other hand, it seems unwise to overnourish him.

In favour of the duel, seriously considered, there are many points to be urged. But the Mensur serves no good purpose whatever. It is childishness, and the fact of its being a cruel and brutal game makes it none the less childish. Wounds have no intrinsic value of their own; it is the cause that dignifies them, not their size. William Tell is rightly one of the heroes of the world; but what should we think of the members of a club of fathers, formed with the object of meeting twice a week to shoot apples from their sons' heads with crossbows? These young German gentlemen could obtain all the results of which they are so proud by teasing a wild cat! To join a society for the mere purpose of getting yourself hacked about reduces a man to the intellectual level of a dancing Dervish. Travellers tell us of savages in Central Africa who express their feelings on festive occasions by jumping about and slashing themselves. But there is no need for Europe to imitate them. The Mensur is, in fact, the *reductio ad absurdum* of the duel; and if the Germans themselves cannot see that it is funny, one can only regret their lack of humour.

But though one may be unable to agree with the public opinion that supports and commands the Mensur, it at least is possible to understand. The University code that, if it does not encourage it, at least condones drunkenness, is more difficult to treat argumentatively. All German students do not get drunk; in fact, the majority are sober, if not industrious. But the minority,

whose claim to be representative is freely admitted, are only
saved from perpetual inebriety by ability, acquired at some cost,
to swill half the day and all the night, while retaining to some
extent their five senses.   It does not affect all alike, but it is
common in any university town to see a young man not yet
twenty with the figure of a Falstaff and the complexion of a
Rubens' Bacchus.   That the German maiden can be fascinated
with a face, cut and gashed till it suggests having been made out
of odd materials that never could have fitted, is a proved fact.
But surely there can be no attraction about a blotched and bloated
skin and a 'bay window' thrown out to an extent threatening to
overbalance the whole structure.   Yet what else can be expected,
when the youngster starts his beer-drinking with a *Fruhschoppen*
at 10 a.m. and closes it with a *Kneipe* at four in the morning?

The *Kneipe* is what we should call a stag party, and can be very
harmless or very rowdy, according to its composition.   One man
invites his fellow-students, a dozen or a hundred, to a café, and
provides them with as much beer and as many cheap cigars as
their own sense of health and comfort may dictate, or the host
may be the Korps itself.   Here, as everywhere, you observe the
German sense of discipline and order.   As each newcomer enters
all those sitting round the table rise, and with heels close together
salute.   When the table is complete, a chairman is chosen, whose
duty it is to give out the number of the songs.   Printed books of
these songs, one to each two men, lie round the table.   The
chairman gives out number twenty-nine.   'First verse,' he cries,
and away all go, each two men holding a book between them
exactly as two people might hold a hymn-book in church.   There
is a pause at the end of each verse until the chairman starts the
company on the next.   As every German is a trained singer,
and as most of them have fair voices, the general effect is striking.

Although the manner may be suggestive of the singing of
hymns in church, the words of the songs are occasionally such as
to correct this impression.   But whether it be a patriotic song, a
sentimental ballad, or a ditty of a nature that would shock the
average young Englishman, all are sung through with stern
earnestness, without a laugh, without a false note.   At the end,
the chairman calls 'Prosit!'   Everyone answers 'Prosit!' and the
next moment every glass is empty.   The pianist rises and bows,
and is bowed to in return; and then the fraulein enters to refill
the glasses.

Between the songs, toasts are proposed and responded to; but there is little cheering, and less laughter. Smiles and grave nods of approval are considered as more seeming among German students.

A particular toast, called a Salamander, accorded to some guest as a special distinction, is drunk with exceptional solemnity.

'We will now,' says the chairman, 'a Salamander rub' ('Einen Salamander reiben'). We all rise, and stand like a regiment at attention.

'Is the stuff prepared?' ('Sind die stoffe parat?') demands the chairman.

'Sunt,' we answer, with one voice.

'Ad exercitium Salamandri,' says the chairman, and we are ready.

'Eins!' We rub our glasses with a circular motion on the table.

'Zwei!' Again the glasses growl; also at 'Drei!'

'Drink!' ('Bibite!')

And with mechanical unison every glass is emptied and held on high.

'Eins!' says the chairman. The foot of every empty glass twirls upon the table, producing a sound as of the dragging back of a stony beach by a receding wave.

'Zwei!' The roll swells and sinks again.

'Drei!' The glasses strike the table with a single crash, and we are in our seats again.

The sport at the *Kneipe* is for two students to insult each other (in play, of course), and to then challenge each other to a drinking duel. An umpire is appointed, two huge glasses are filled, and the men sit opposite each other with their hands upon the handles, all eyes fixed upon them. The umpire gives the word to go, and in an instant the beer is gurgling down their throats. The man who bangs his perfectly finished glass upon the table first is victor.

Strangers who are going through a *Kneipe*, and who wish to do the thing in German style, will do well, before commencing proceedings, to pin their name and address upon their coats. The German student is courtesy itself, and whatever his own state may be, he will see to it that, by some means or another, his guests get safely home before the morning. But, of course, he cannot be expected to remember addresses.

A story was told me of three guests to a Berlin *Kneipe* which might have had tragic results. The strangers determined to do the thing thoroughly. They explained their intention, and were applauded, and each proceeded to write his address upon his card, and pin it to the tablecloth in front of him. That was the mistake they made. They should, as I have advised, have pinned it carefully to their coats. A man may change his place at a table, quite unconsciously he may come out the other side of it; but wherever he goes he takes his coat with him.

Some time in the small hours, the chairman suggested that to make things more comfortable for those still upright, all the gentlemen unable to keep their heads off the table should be sent home. Among those to whom the proceedings had become uninteresting were the three Englishmen. It was decided to put them into a cab in charge of a comparatively speaking sober student, and return them. Had they retained their original seats throughout the evening all would have been well; but, unfortunately, they had gone walking about, and which gentleman belonged to which card nobody knew—least of all the guests themselves. In the then state of general cheerfulness, this did not to anybody appear to much matter. There were three gentlemen and three addresses. I suppose the idea was that even if a mistake were made, the parties could be sorted out in the morning. Anyhow, the three gentlemen were put into a cab, the comparatively speaking sober student took the three cards in his hand, and the party started amid the cheers and good wishes of the company.

There is this advantage about German beer: it does not make a man drunk as the word drunk is understood in England. There is nothing objectionable about him; he is simply tired. He does not want to talk; he wants to be let alone, to go to sleep; it does not matter where—anywhere.

The conductor of the party stopped his cab at the nearest address. He took out his worst case; it was a natural instinct to get rid of that first. He and the cabman carried it upstairs, and rang the bell of the *pension*. A sleepy porter answered it. They carried their burden in, and looked for a place to drop it. A bedroom door happened to be open; the room was empty; could anything be better?—they took it in there. They relieved it of such things as came off easily, and laid it in the bed. This done, both men, pleased with themselves, returned to the cab.

At the next address they stopped again. This time, in answer to their summons, a lady appeared, dressed in a tea-gown, with a book in her hand. The German student looked at the top one of two cards remaining in his hand, and inquired if he had the pleasure of addressing Frau Y. It happened that he had, though so far as any pleasure was concerned that appeared to be entirely on his side. He explained to Frau Y that the gentleman at that moment asleep against the wall was her husband. The reunion moved her to no enthusiasm; she simply opened the bedroom door, and then walked away. The cabman and the student took him in, and laid him on the bed. They did not trouble to undress him; they were feeling tired! They did not see the lady of the house again, and retired therefore without adeius.

He explains that that is her husband

The last card was that of a bachelor stopping at an hotel. They took their last man, therefore, to that hotel, passed him over to the night porter, and left him.

To return to the address at which the first delivery was made, what had happened there was this. Some eight hours previously had said Mr X to Mrs X: 'I think I told you, my dear, that I had an invitation for this evening to what, I believe, is called a *Kneipe*?'

'You did mention something of the sort,' replied Mrs X. 'What is a *Kneipe*?'

'Well, it's a sort of bachelor party, my dear, where the students meet to sing and talk and—and smoke, and all that sort of thing, you know.'

'Oh well, I hope you will enjoy yourself!' said Mrs X, who was a nice woman and sensible.

'It will be interesting,' observed Mr X. 'I have often had a curiosity to see one. I may,' continued Mr X—'I mean it is possible that I may be home a little late.'

'What do you call late?' asked Mrs X.

'It is somewhat difficult to say,' returned Mr X. 'You see these students, they are a wild lot, and when they get together—— And then, I believe, a good many toasts are drunk. I don't know how it will affect me. If I can see an opportunity I shall come away early, that is if I can do so without giving offence; but if not——'

Said Mrs X, who, as I remarked before, was a sensible woman: 'You had better get the people here to lend you a latch-key. I shall sleep with Dolly, and then you won't disturb me whatever time it may be.'

'I think that an excellent idea of yours,' agreed Mr X. 'I should hate disturbing you. I shall just come in quietly, and slip into bed.'

Some time in the middle of the night, or maybe towards the early morning, Dolly, who was Mrs X's sister, sat up in bed and listened.

'Jenny,' said Dolly, 'are you awake?'

'Yes, dear,' answered Mrs X. 'It's all right. You go to sleep again.'

'But whatever is it?' asked Dolly. 'Do you think it's fire?'

'I expect,' replied Mrs X, 'that it's Percy. Very possibly he has stumbled over something in the dark. Don't you worry, dear; you go to sleep.'

But so soon as Dolly had dozed off again, Mrs X, who was a good wife, thought she would steal off softly and see to it that Percy was all right. So, putting on a dressing-gown and slippers, she crept along the passage and into her own room. To awake the gentleman on the bed would have required an earthquake. She lit a candle and stole over to the bedside.

It was not Percy; it was not anyone like Percy. She felt it was not the man that ever could have been her husband under any circumstances. In his present condition her sentiment towards him was that of positive dislike. Her only desire was to get rid of him.

But something there was about him which seemed familiar to her. She went nearer, and took a closer view. Then she remembered.   Surely it was Mr Y, a gentleman at whose flat she and Percy had dined the day they first arrived in Berlin.

But what was he doing here?   She put the candle on the table, and taking her head between her hands sat down to think.   The explanation of the thing came to her with a rush.   It was with this Mr Y that Percy had gone to the *Kneipe*.   A mistake had been made.   Mr Y had been brought back to Percy's address. Percy at this very moment——

The terrible possibilities of the situation swam before her. Returning to Dolly's room, she dressed herself hastily, and silently crept downstairs.   Finding, fortunately, a passing night-cab, she drove to the address of Mrs Y.   Telling the man to wait, she flew upstairs and rang persistently at the bell.   It was opened as before by Mrs Y, still in her tea-gown, and with her book still in her hand.

'Mrs X!' exclaimed Mrs Y.   'Whatever brings you here?'

'My husband!' was all poor Mrs X could think to say at the moment, 'is he here?'

'Mrs X,' returned Mrs Y, drawing herself up to her full height, 'how dare you?'

'Oh, please don't misunderstand me!' pleaded Mrs X.   'It's all a terrible mistake.   They must have brought poor Percy here instead of to our place, I'm sure they must.   Do please look and see.'

'My dear,' said Mrs Y, who was a much older woman, and more motherly, 'don't excite yourself.   They brought him here about half an hour ago, and, to tell you the truth, I never looked at him.   He is in here.   I don't think they troubled to take off even his boots.   If you keep cool, we will get him downstairs and home without a soul beyond ourselves being any the wiser.'

Indeed, Mrs Y seemed quite eager to help Mrs X.

She pushed open the door, and Mrs X went in.   The next moment she came out with a white, scared face.

'It isn't Percy,' she said.   'Whatever am I to do?'

'I wish you wouldn't make these mistakes,' said Mrs Y, moving to enter the room herself.

Mrs X stopped her.   'And it isn't your husband either.'

'Nonsense,' said Mrs Y.

'It isn't really,' persisted Mrs X.   'I know, because I have just left him, asleep on Percy's bed.'

'What's he doing there?' thundered Mrs Y.

'They brought him there, and put him there,' explained Mrs

X, beginning to cry. 'That's what made me think Percy must be here.'

The two women stood and looked at one another; and there was silence for a while, broken only by the snoring of the gentleman the other side of the half-open door.

'Then who is that, in there?' demanded Mrs Y, who was the first to recover herself.

'I don't know,' answered Mrs X, 'I have never seen him before. Do you think it is anybody you know?'

But Mrs Y only banged-to the door.

'What are we to do?' said Mrs X.

'I know what *I* am going to do,' said Mrs Y. 'I'm coming back with you to fetch my husband.'

'He's very sleepy,' explained Mrs X.

'I've known him to be that before,' replied Mrs Y, as she fastened on her cloak.

'But where's Percy?' sobbed poor little Mrs X, as they descended the stairs together.

'That, my dear,' said Mrs Y, 'will be a question for you to ask *him*.'

'If they go about making mistakes like this,' said Mrs X, 'it is impossible to say what they may not have done with him.'

'We will make inquiries in the morning, my dear,' said Mrs Y, consolingly.

'I think these *Kneipes* are disgraceful affairs,' said Mrs X. 'I shall never let Percy go to another, never—so long as I live.'

'My dear,' remarked Mrs Y, 'if you know your duty, he will never want to.' And rumour has it that he never did.

But, as I have said, the mistake was in pinning the card to the tablecloth instead of to the coat. And error in this world is always severely punished.

CHAPTER XIV

*Which is serious: as becomes a parting chapter—The German from the
Anglo-Saxon's point of view—Providence in buttons and a helmet—
Paradise of the helpless idiot—German conscience: its aggressiveness—
How they hang in Germany, very possibly—What happens to good
Germans when they die?—The military instinct: is it all-sufficient?—
The German as a shopkeeper—How he supports life—The New
Woman, here as everywhere—What can be said against the Germans,
as a people—The Bummel is over and done.*

'ANYBODY could rule this country,' said George; '*I* could rule it.'

We were seated in the garden of the Kaiser Hof at Bonn,
looking down upon the Rhine. It was the last evening of our
Bummel; the early morning train would be the beginning of the
end.

'I should write down all I wanted the people to do on a piece
of paper,' continued George; 'get a good firm to print off so
many copies, have them posted about the towns and villages; and
the thing would be done.'

In the placid, docile German of to-day, whose only ambition
appears to be to pay his taxes, and do what he is told to do by
those whom it has pleased Providence to place in authority over
him, it is difficult, one must confess, to detect any trace of his
wild ancestor, to whom individual liberty was as the breath of his
nostrils; who appointed his magistrates to advise, but retained
the right of execution for the tribe; who followed his chief, but
would have scorned to obey him. In Germany to-day one hears
a good deal concerning Socialism, but it is a Socialism that would
only be despotism under another name. Individualism makes
no appeal to the German voter. He is willing, nay, anxious, to
be controlled and regulated in all things. He disputes, not
government, but the form of it. The policeman is to him a
religion, and, one feels, will always remain so. In England we
regard our man in blue as a harmless necessity. By the average
citizen he is employed chiefly as a signpost, though in busy
quarters of the town he is considered useful for taking old ladies
across the road. Beyond feeling thankful to him for these
services, I doubt if we take much thought of him. In Germany,

on the other hand, he is worshipped as a little god and loved as a guardian angel. To the German child he is a combination of Santa Claus and the Bogie Man. All good things come from him: Spielplätze to play in, furnished with swings and giant-strides, sand heaps to fight around, swimming baths, and fairs. All misbehaviour is punished by him. It is the hope of every well-meaning German boy and girl to please the police. To be smiled at by a policeman makes it conceited. A German child that has been patted on the head by a policeman is not fit to live with; its self-importance is unbearable.

The German child that is patted by a policeman

The German citizen is a soldier, and the policeman is his officer. The policeman directs him where in the street to walk, and how fast to walk. At the end of each bridge stands a policeman to tell the German how to cross it. Were there no policeman there, he would probably sit down and wait till the river had passed by. At the railway station the policeman locks him up in the waiting-room, where he can do no harm to himself. When the proper time arrives, he fetches him out and hands him over to the guard of the train, who is only a policeman in another uniform. The guard tells him where to sit in the train, and when to get out, and sees that he does get out. In Germany you take no responsibility upon yourself whatever. Everything is done for you, and done well. You are not supposed to look after yourself; you are not blamed for being incapable of looking after yourself; it is the duty of the German policeman to look after you. That you may be a helpless idiot does not excuse him should anything happen to you. Wherever you are and whatever you are doing you are in his charge, and he takes care of you—good care of you; there is no denying this.

If you lose yourself, he finds you; and if you lose anything belonging to you, he recovers it for you. If you don't know what you want, he tells you. If you want anything that is good for you to have, he gets it for you. Private lawyers are not needed in Germany. If you want to buy or sell a house or field, the State makes out the conveyance. If you have been swindled, the State takes up the case for you. The State marries you, insures you, will even gamble with you for a trifle.

'You get yourself born,' says the German Government to the German citizen, 'we do the rest. Indoors and out of doors, in sickness and in health, in pleasure and in work, we will tell you what to do, and we will see to it that you do it. Don't you worry yourself about anything.'

And the German doesn't. Where there is no policeman to be found, he wanders about till he comes to a police notice posted on a wall. This he reads; then he goes and does what it says.

I remember in one German town—I forget which; it is immaterial; the incident could have happened in any—noticing an open gate leading to a garden in which a concert was being given. There was nothing to prevent anyone who chose from walking through that gate, and thus gaining admittance to the concert without paying. In fact, of the two gates a quarter of a mile apart it was the more convenient. Yet of the crowds that passed, not one attempted to enter by that gate. They plodded steadily on under a blazing sun to the other gate, at which a man stood to collect the entrance money. I have seen German youngsters stand longingly by the margin of a lonely sheet of ice. They could have skated on that ice for hours, and nobody have been the wiser. The crowd and the police were at the other end, more than half a mile away, and round the corner. Nothing stopped their going on but the knowledge that they ought not. Things such as these make one pause to seriously wonder whether the Teuton be a member of the sinful human family or not. Is it not possible that these placid, gentle folk may in reality be angels, come down to earth for the sake of a glass of beer, which, as they must know, can only in Germany be obtained worth the drinking?

In Germany the country roads are lined with fruit trees. There is no voice to stay man or boy from picking and eating the fruit, except conscience. In England such a state of things would cause public indignation. Children would die of cholera by the hundred. The medical profession would be worked off its legs trying to cope with the natural results of over-indulgence in sour apples and unripe walnuts. Public opinion would demand that these fruit trees should be fenced about, and thus rendered harmless. Fruit growers, to save themselves the expense of walls and palings, would not be allowed in this manner to spread sickness and death throughout the community.

But in Germany a boy will walk for miles down a lonely road, hedged with fruit trees, to buy a pennyworth of pears in the village at the other end. To pass these unprotected fruit trees, drooping under their burden of ripe fruit, strikes the Anglo-Saxon mind as a wicked waste of opportunity, a flouting of the blessed gifts of Providence.

I do not know if it be so, but from what I have observed of the German character I should not be surprised to hear that when a man in Germany is condemned to death he is given a piece of rope, and told to go and hang himself. It would save the State much trouble and expense, and I can see that German criminal taking that piece of rope home with him, reading up carefully the police instructions, and proceeding to carry them out in his own back kitchen.

The Germans are a good people. On the whole, the best people perhaps in the world; an amiable, unselfish, kindly people. I am positive that the vast majority of them go to heaven. Indeed, comparing them with the other Christian nations of the earth, one is forced to the conclusion that heaven will be chiefly of German manufacture. But I cannot understand how they get there. That the soul of any single individual German has sufficient initiative to fly up by itself and knock at St Peter's door, I cannot believe. My own opinion is that they are taken there in small companies, and passed in under the charge of a dead policeman.

Carlyle said of the Prussians, and it is true of the whole German nation, that one of their chief virtues was their power of being drilled. Of the Germans you might say they are a people who will go anywhere, and do anything, they are told. Drill him for the work and send him out to Africa or Asia under charge of somebody in uniform, and he is bound to make an excellent colonist, facing difficulties as he would face the devil himself, if ordered. But it is not easy to conceive of him as a pioneer. Left to run himself, one feels he would soon fade away and die, not from any lack of intelligence, but from sheer want of presumption.

The German has so long been the soldier of Europe, that the

Reading carefully the instructions

military instinct has entered into his blood. The military virtues he possesses in abundance; but he also suffers from the drawbacks of the military training. It was told me of a German servant, lately released from the barracks, that he was instructed by his master to deliver a letter to a certain house, and to wait there for the answer. The hours passed by, and the man did not return. His master, anxious and surprised, followed. He found the man where he had been sent, the answer in his hand. He was waiting for further orders. The story sounds exaggerated, but personally I can credit it.

The curious thing is that the same man, who as an individual is as helpless as a child, becomes, the moment he puts on the uniform, an intelligent being, capable of responsibility and initiative. The German can rule others, and be ruled by others, but he cannot rule himself. The cure would appear to be to train every German for an officer, and then put him under himself. It is certain he would order himself about with discretion and judgment, and see to it that he himself obeyed himself with smartness and precision.

For the direction of German character into these channels, the schools, of course, are chiefly responsible. Their everlasting teaching is duty. It is a fine ideal for any people; but before buckling to it, one would wish to have a clear understanding as to what his 'duty' is. The German idea of it would appear to be: 'blind obedience to everything in buttons.' It is the antithesis of the Anglo-Saxon scheme; but as both the Anglo-Saxon and the Teuton are prospering, there must be good in both methods. Hitherto, the German has had the blessed fortune to be exceptionally well governed; if this continue, it will go well with him. When his troubles will begin will be when by any chance something goes wrong with the governing machine. But maybe his method has the advantage of producing a continuous supply of good governors; it would certainly seem so.

As a trader, I am inclined to think the German will, unless his temperament considerably change, remain always a long way behind his Anglo-Saxon competitor; and this by reason of his virtues. To him life is something more important than a mere race for wealth. A country that closes its banks and post-offices for two hours in the middle of the day, while it goes home and enjoys a comfortable meal in the bosom of its family, with, perhaps, forty winks by way of dessert, cannot hope, and possibly has no wish, to compete with a people that takes its meals standing, and sleeps with a telephone over its bed.   In Germany there is not, at all events as yet, sufficient distinction between the classes to make the struggle for position the life and death affair it is in England.   Beyond the landed aristocracy, whose boundaries are impregnable, grade hardly counts.   Frau Professor and Frau Candlestickmaker meet at the weekly *Kaffee-Klatsch* and exchange scandal on terms of mutual equality.   The livery-stable keeper and the doctor hobnob together at their favourite beer hall.   The wealthy master builder, when he prepares his roomy wagon for an excursion into the country, invites his foreman and his tailor to join him with their families.   Each brings his share of drink and provisions, and returning home they sing in chorus the same songs.   So long as this state of things endures, a man is not induced to sacrifice the best years of his life to win a fortune for his dotage.   His tastes, and, more to the point still, his wife's, remain inexpensive.   He likes to see his flat or villa furnished with much red plush upholstery and a profusion of gilt and lacquer.   But this is his idea; and maybe it is in no worse taste than is a mixture of bastard Elizabethan with imitation Louis XV, the whole lit by electric light, and smothered with photographs.   Possibly, he will have his outer walls painted by the local artist: a sanguinary battle, a good deal interfered with by the front door, taking place below, while Bismarck, as an angel, flutters vaguely about the bedroom windows.   But for his Old Masters he is quite content to go to the public galleries; and 'the Celebrity at Home' not having as yet taken its place amongst the institutions of the Fatherland, he is not impelled to waste his money turning his house into an old curiosity shop.

The German is a gourmand.   There are still English farmers who, while telling you that farming spells starvation, enjoy their seven solid meals a day.   Once a year there comes a week's feast throughout Russia, during which many deaths occur from the overeating of pancakes; but this is a religious festival, and an exception.   Taking him all round, the German as a trencherman stands pre-eminent among the nations of the earth.   He rises early, and while dressing tosses off a few cups of coffee, together with half a dozen hot buttered rolls.   But it is not until ten o'clock that he sits down to anything that can properly be called a meal.   At one or half past takes place his chief dinner.   Of this he makes a business, sitting at it for a couple of hours.   At four o'clock he goes to the café, and eats cakes and drinks chocolate.

The evening he devotes to eating generally—not a set meal, or rarely, but a series of snacks—a bottle of beer and a Belegete-semmel or two at seven, say; another bottle of beer and an Aufschnitt at the theatre between the acts; a small bottle of white wine and a Spiegeleier before going home; then a piece of cheese or sausage, washed down by more beer, previous to turning in for the night.

But he is no gourmet. French cooks and French prices are not the rule at his restaurant. His beer or his inexpensive native white wine he prefers to the most costly clarets or champagnes. And, indeed, it is well for him he does; for one is inclined to think that every time a French grower sells a bottle of wine to a German hotel or shopkeeper, Sedan is rankling in his mind. It is a foolish revenge, seeing that it is not the German who as a rule drinks it; the punishment falls upon some innocent travel-ling Englishman. Maybe, however, the French dealer remem-bers also Waterloo, and feels that in any event he scores.

In Germany expensive entertainments are neither offered nor expected. Everything throughout the Fatherland is homely and friendly. The German has no costly sports to pay for, no showy establishment to maintain, no purse-proud circle to dress for. His chief pleasure, a seat at the opera or concert, can be had for a few marks; and his wife and daughters walk there in home-made dresses, with shawls over their heads. Indeed, throughout the country the absence of all ostentation is to English eyes quite refreshing. Private carriages are few and far between, and even the droshky is made use of only when the quicker and cleaner electric car is not available.

By such means the German retains his independence. The shopkeeper in Germany does not fawn upon his customers. I accompanied an English lady once on a shopping excursion in Munich. She had been accustomed to shopping in London and New York, and she grumbled at everything the man showed her. It was not that she was really dissatisfied; this was her method. She explained that she could get most things cheaper and better elsewhere; not that she really thought she could, merely she held it good for the shopkeeper to say this. She told him that his stock lacked taste—she did not mean to be offensive; as I have explained, it was her method—that there was no variety about it; that it was not up to date; that it was commonplace; that it looked as if it would not wear. He did not argue with her; he did not contradict her. He put the things back into their respective boxes, replaced the boxes on their respective shelves, walked into the little parlour behind the shop, and closed the door.

'Isn't he ever coming back?' asked the lady, after a couple of minutes had elapsed.

Her tone did not imply a question so much as an exclamation of mere impatience.

'I doubt it,' I replied.

'Why not?' she asked, much astonished.

'I expect,' I answered, 'you have bored him. In all probability he is at this moment behind that door smoking a pipe and reading the paper.'

'What an extraordinary shopkeeper!' said my friend, as she gathered her parcels together and indignantly walked out.

'It is their way,' I explained. 'There are the goods; if you want them, you can have them. If you do not want them, they would almost rather that you did not come and talk about them.'

On another occasion I listened in the smoke-room of a German hotel to a small Englishman telling a tale which, had I been in his place, I should have kept to myself.

'It doesn't do,' said the little Englishman, 'to try and beat a German down. They don't seem to understand it. I saw a first edition of *The Robbers* in a shop in the Georg Platz. I went in and asked the price. It was a rum old chap behind the counter. He said: "Twenty-five marks," and went on reading. I told him I had seen a better copy only a few days before for twenty—one talks like that when one is bargaining; it is understood. He asked me "Where?" I told him in a shop at Leipzig. He suggested my returning there and getting it; he did not seem to care whether I bought the book or whether I didn't. I said:

'"What's the least you will take for it?"

'"I have told you once," he answered; "twenty-five marks." He was an irritable old chap.

'I said: "It's not worth it."

'"I never said it was, did I?" he snapped.

'I said: "I'll give you ten marks for it." I thought, maybe, he would end by taking twenty.

'He rose. I took it he was coming round the counter to get the book out. Instead, he came straight up to me. He was a biggish sort of man. He took me by the two shoulders, walked me out into the street, and closed the door behind me with a bang. I was never more surprised in all my life.'

'Maybe the book was worth twenty-five marks,' I suggested.

'Of course it was,' he replied; 'well worth it. But what a notion of business!'

If anything can change the German character, it will be the German woman. She herself is changing rapidly—advancing, as we call it. Ten years ago no German woman caring for her reputation, hoping for a husband, would have dared to ride a bicycle: to-day they spin about the country in their thousands. The old folks shake their heads at them; but the young men, I notice, overtake them and ride beside them. Not long ago it was considered unwomanly in Germany for a lady to be able to do the outside edge. Her proper skating attitude was thought to be that of clinging limpness to some male relative. Now she practises eights in a corner by herself, until some young man comes along to help her. She plays tennis, and, from a point of safety, I have even noticed her driving a dog-cart.

Brilliantly educated she always has been. At eighteen she speaks two or three languages, and has forgotten more than the average Englishwoman has ever read. Hitherto, this education has been utterly useless to her. On marriage she has retired into the kitchen, and made haste to clear her brain of everything else, in order to leave room for bad cooking. But suppose it begins to dawn upon her that a woman need not sacrifice her whole existence to household drudgery any more than a man need make himself nothing else than a business machine. Suppose she develop an ambition to take part in the social and national life. Then the influence of such a partner, healthy in body and therefore vigorous in mind, is bound to be both lasting and far-reaching.

For it must be borne in mind that the German man is exceptionally sentimental, and most easily influenced by his women-folk. It is said of him, he is the best of lovers, the worst of husbands. This has been the woman's fault. Once married, the German woman has done more than put romance behind her; she has taken a carpet-beater and driven it out of the house. As a girl, she never understood dressing; as a wife, she takes off such clothes even as she had, and proceeds to wrap herself up in any odd articles she may happen to find about the house; at all events, this is the impression she produces. The figure that might often be that of a Juno, the complexion that would sometimes do credit to a healthy angel, she proceeds of malice and intent to spoil. She sells her birthright of admiration and devotion for a mess of sweets. Every afternoon you may see her at the café, loading herself with rich cream-covered cakes, washed down by copious draughts of chocolate. In a short time she becomes fat, pasty, placid, and utterly uninteresting.

When the German woman gives up her afternoon coffee and her evening beer, takes sufficient exercise to retain her shape, and continues to read after marriage something else than the cookery book, the German Government will find it has a new and unknown force to deal with. And everywhere throughout Germany one is confronted by unmistakable signs that the old German Frauen are giving place to the newer Damen.

Concerning what will then happen one feels curious. For the German nation is still young, and its maturity is of importance to the world. They are a good people, a lovable people, who should help much to make the world better.

The worst that can be said against them is that they have their failings. They themselves do no know this; they consider themselves perfect, which is foolish of them. They even go so far as to think themselves superior to the Anglo-Saxon: this is incomprehensible. One feels they must be pretending.

'They have their points,' said George; 'but their tobacco is a national sin. I'm going to bed.'

We rose, and leaning over the low stone parapet, watched the dancing lights upon the soft, dark river.

'It has been a pleasant Bummel, on the whole,' said Harris; 'I shall be glad to get back, and yet I am sorry it is over, if you understand me.'

"What is a "Bummel"?' said George. 'How would you translate it?'

'A "Bummel,"' I explained, 'I should describe as a journey, long or short, without an end; the only thing regulating it being the necessity of getting back within a given time to the point from which one started. Sometimes it is through busy streets, and sometimes through the fields and lanes; sometimes we can be spared for a few hours, and sometimes for a few days. But long or short, but here or there, our thoughts are ever on the running of the sand. We nod and smile to many as we pass; with some we stop and talk awhile; and with a few we walk a little way. We have been much interested, and often a little tired. But on the whole we have had a pleasant time, and are sorry when 'tis over.'